¿Quién manda en los bosques?

Interacciones en un ecosistema

Autora: **Yu-Jeong Lee**   Ilustradora: **Ye-Jeong Cho**   Asesora: **Eun-Ju Lee**

Altea

En un lugar remoto había una porción
de tierra que no tenía dueño.
Era una tierra que nadie quería
ni cuidaba, por eso estaba
seca y descuidada.

Durante mucho tiempo, la tierra tuvo que
sobrevivir sola.

Un día, el Sol llamó al viento
y a la lluvia para alegrar a
la abandonada y sombría tierra.
Primero, el viento sopló desde la lejanía
trayendo semillas con él.
Luego, la lluvia cayó a cántaros sobre ella.

La tierra seca se empapó.
Las semillas penetraron en ella,
el Sol la bañó con sus cálidos rayos;
luego las semillas echaron raíces,
una por una.
El viento sopló su aliento sobre
las semillas y brotaron
retoños de la tierra.
La tierra pronto se cubrió
de tréboles.

Pasó un año.
Los pastos altos eclipsaron
a los pastos cortos y al instante éstos
cedieron su lugar.
El pasto alto atrajo insectos y bichos
que cuidaron activamente la tierra.
De este modo empezó a formarse ahí
un suelo fértil.

Los árboles también querían vivir
en los campos soleados, cálidos,
extensos y verdes.

La primera semilla en llegar fue la del pino,
que batía sus alas mientras volaba
con el viento.

Los jóvenes pinos
crecieron,
crecieron...
y crecieron aún más.
Y entonces...

Nació un bosque lleno de
coníferas.

Las coníferas...
Son árboles que
tienen hojas
en forma de aguja.
Los pinos y los abetos
son coníferas.
Su madera es dura y
resistente, y suele
usarse como material
de construcción.
Crecen en regiones
tibias o frías, y la
mayoría de las coníferas
son de hoja perenne,
de modo que están
verdes todo el año.

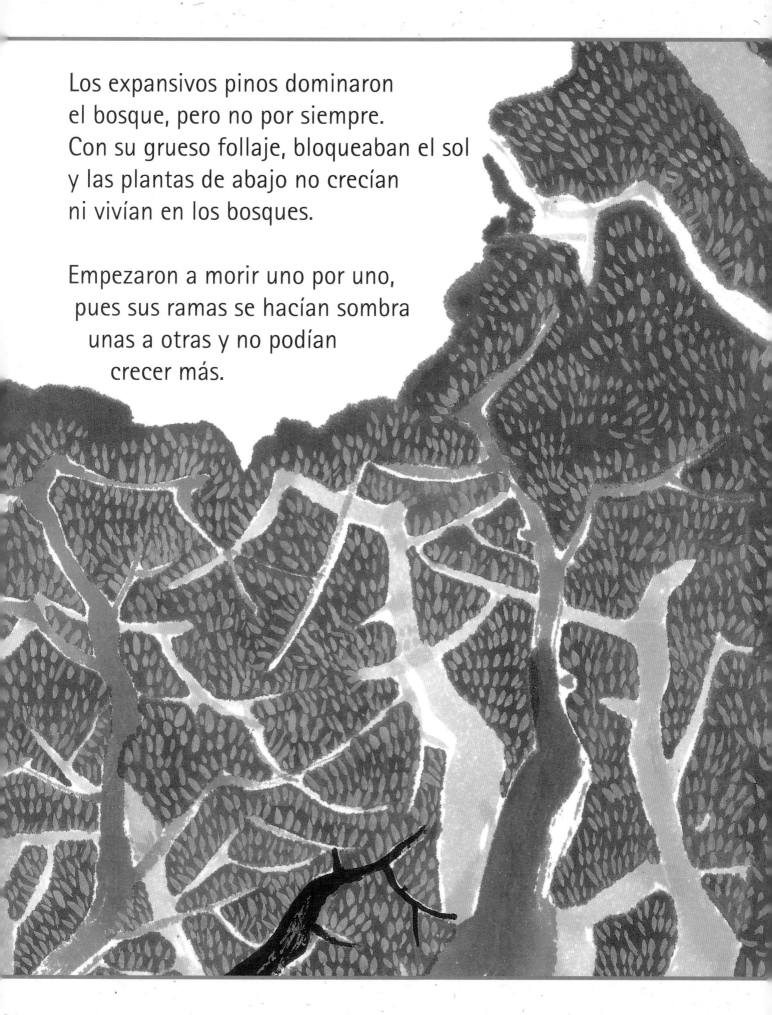

Los expansivos pinos dominaron
el bosque, pero no por siempre.
Con su grueso follaje, bloqueaban el sol
y las plantas de abajo no crecían
ni vivían en los bosques.

Empezaron a morir uno por uno,
pues sus ramas se hacían sombra
unas a otras y no podían
crecer más.

Durante este tiempo, los árboles
de hoja ancha retoñaron
y comenzaron a crecer.

Árboles de hoja ancha...
Son árboles con hojas en forma
de abanico. El roble, el encino,
la morera y la *paulownia* son
algunos de estos árboles.
El grano de su madera es tan
hermoso que a menudo se usa
para hacer muebles.
Hay dos tipos de árboles de hoja
ancha: los perennes, que no
pierden sus hojas en otoño, y
los de hoja caduca, que sí las
pierden. Estos árboles viven en
regiones cálidas y tropicales.

Los árboles jóvenes extienden sus ramas, que se cubren con muchas hojas anchas, hacia el cielo. Entierran sus fuertes raíces en lo más hondo de la tierra.

Los que no han terminado de crecer compiten por ver cuál crecerá más alto. Al principio, el hermoso arce lleno de hojas parecía que iba a ganar, pero el encino produce muchas bellotas y extiende sus ramas muy alto.
El roble y el carpe están ocupados en hacer crecer hojas nuevas.

Los animales se entusiasmaron cuando oyeron que los árboles estaban compitiendo.
Esto quería decir que podrían comer sus hojas tiernas y jugosas, así como sus frutos, hasta hartarse y dormir calientes entre sus ramas o usar las hojas como cobertores.

En los bosques hay...
Muchos animales silvestres. En los bosques también podemos encontrar raíces y champiñones, que son buenos para la salud.

La tierra descuidada y seca que antes nadie quería
ni cuidaba se ha convertido en un gran bosque.
Ahora, los árboles de este bosque compiten por dominarlo.

Cuanto más compiten, más exuberante
y hermoso se hace el bosque.

Los bosques...
Limpian el aire. Porque la gran
cantidad de árboles que hay en los
bosques absorben el dañino dióxido
de carbono y liberan oxígeno
a través de sus hojas.

También muestran
a la gente
la belleza y la
comodidad que
la naturaleza
puede brindar.

24

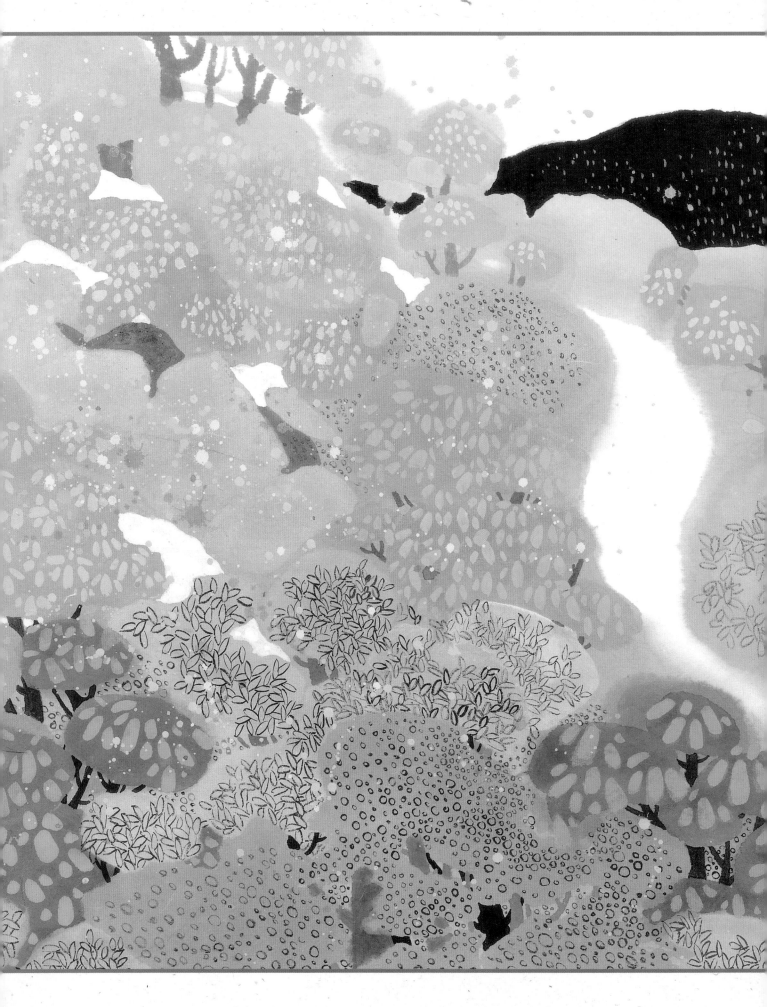

Los árboles siguen compitiendo
entre sí para dominar los bosques.

Los bosques...
Evitan que la tierra se erosione por las fuertes
lluvias, porque los árboles entierran hondo
sus raíces en la tierra.
También de los bosques obtenemos pulpa,
que es la materia prima para hacer papel.

Nota de la profesora

¿Quién manda en los bosques?

Eun-Ju Lee (Universidad de Seúl, Facultad de Ciencias Naturales)

El 28 de marzo de 1982, un volcán empezó a hacer erupción en Chiapas, México. Continuó haciendo erupción hasta el 4 de abril, cuando produjo una columna de ceniza y humo que llegó a la estratósfera.

Debido a este cataclismo, desaparecieron plantaciones de plátano, cacao, café y otros cultivos. Éstas se cubrieron de ceniza volcánica, lo que significó que durante un tiempo no se encontraran organismos vivos.

Sin embargo, al paso de los años, comenzaron a aparecer organismos en ese lugar. Al principio crecieron plantas pequeñas. Luego volaron algunas aves desde los alrededores, trayendo consigo semillas que depositaron en sus excreciones, y después también llegaron semillas arrastradas por el viento. Paulatinamente, un sinnúmero de insectos y árboles llegaron a la isla y empezaron a crecer. Pasaron décadas y el bosque se restauró llegando a ser lo que alguna vez fue en el pasado.

El proceso por el que las plantas crecen en un lugar conforme pasa el tiempo y luego cambian, se llama "sucesión ecológica". Existen la sucesión primaria y la secundaria. La primaria es cuando seres vivos se mudan a un lugar en el que no ha habido otros seres vivos y empiezan a desarrollarse ahí. La secundaria es cuando el ambiente es destruido: por ejemplo, un bosque que se quema en las montañas y las plantas se adaptan a los cambios. Normalmente, la sucesión secundaria ocurre a una velocidad mucho mayor que la primaria. La razón es que en el suelo hay un rico abasto de nutrientes y permanecen algunas semillas, plantas y animales, de modo que éste se recupera con rapidez.

Durante el periodo Devónico, la competencia por el espacio y la luz provocó que las plantas empezaran a crecer hacia arriba. Entonces los árboles como el pino y el abedul crecieron y llenaron los bosques. Sin embargo, estos árboles crecen bien al sol cuando son jóvenes, pero no así en la sombra. Finalmente, el arce, el carpe y el abeto, que sobreviven bien a la sombra, dominaron el bosque.

La tierra ocupa aproximadamente 30% de la superficie terrestre. El bosque es hogar de muchos animales silvestres y proporciona una enorme ganancia ambiental y económica.

El bosque purifica el aire desde el punto de vista ambiental y produce oxígeno, que es esencial para la vida. Asimismo, si llueve demasiado, reduce la posibilidad de inundaciones, pues el agua fluye poco a poco bajo tierra a través de los árboles. También protege los suelos, evitando que se deslaven. Económicamente, el bosque nos provee madera para construir casas y pulpa para hacer papel. A veces se producen champiñones y frutos deliciosos, así como carbón.

Si en verano te paras cerca del magnífico bosque sentirás su frescura. Los bosques sustentan mucha vida silvestre y son un lugar donde podemos descansar y relajarnos en paz. Sería genial que cuidáramos los bosques y viviéramos en armonía con ellos.

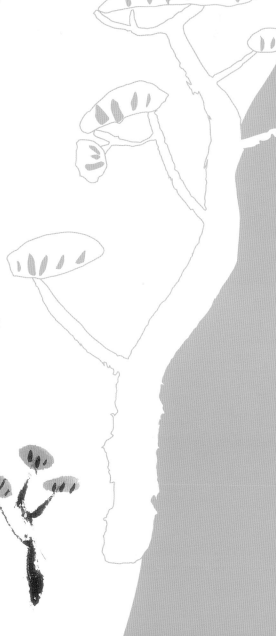

La autora, **Yu-Jeong Lee,** se graduó en la Universidad Chung-Ang en Literatura Creativa. También escribe, diseña escenarios para personajes animados, hace versos para niños, historias y otros relatos.

La ilustradora, **Ye-Jeong Cho,** estudió en la Universidad Chung-Ang. Participa activamente en un grupo que realiza estudios de investigación sobre historias para niños, y se dedica a la ilustración de libros. Ha ilustrado, entre otros, *Jack and the Bean Stalk, Dream of an Anchovy King, Goblin and the Spring Wind.*

La asesora, **Eun-Ju Lee,** se graduó en la Universidad Nacional de Seúl, con especialidad en Botánica, y recibió asimismo el grado de maestría. Se especializó también en botánica en la Universidad de Manitoba, Canadá. Es profesora de Ciencia de la Vida en la Universidad Nacional de Seúl. Le encantan los libros para niños, y le gustaría que los pequeños se interesaran más en las plantas y en la vegetación, que son los cimientos de la vida.

Altea

¿Quién manda en los bosques? Interacciones en un ecosistema | ISBN: 978-970-770-877-8
Título original: *Who is the Ruler of the Wood* | D.R. © Yeowon Media, 2006 |
De la primera edición en español: D.R. © Santillana Ediciones Generales, S.A. de C.V., 2007,
Av. Universidad 767, Col. Del Valle, México, D.F. | Coordinación editorial: Gerardo Mendiola |
Traducción y formación: Alquimia Ediciones, S.A. de C.V. | Cuidado de la edición: Carlos Tejada,
Gerardo Mendiola y Norma Fernández Guerrero |

De esta edición: D.R. © Santillana USA Publishing Company, Inc., 2012.
2023 NW 84th Ave., Doral, FL 33178

www.santillanausa.com

Make a Joyful Noise!

Music, Movement, and Creative Play
to Teach Bible Stories

Preschool–Grade 1

by Kathryn Nider Wolf & Heather P. Robbins

NEW DAY
PUBLISHING

Greensboro, North Carolina
886-763-2977 order line
www.newdaypublishing.net

Make a Joyful Noise!
Music, Movement, and Creative Play to Teach Bible Stories

Authors: Kathryn Nider Wolf & Heather P. Robbins

Design & Illustrations: Jennifer Tipton Cappoen

Editor: Annie Galvin Teich

ISBN 978-0-9789056-8-2

Publisher: New Day Publishing, Inc., Greensboro, North Carolina

Table of Contents

Editors Note: * indicates songs and finger plays featured on the *Make a Joyful Noise!* CD ©2007 New Day Publishing, Inc.

How to Use This Book

Music, movement, and creative dramatics – all play an important role in early childhood development. What appears to be "play" is actually important work as children develop a variety of physical, cognitive, language, social, and emotional skills. *Make a Joyful Noise!* provides fun, easy-to-implement activities based on the developmental skills and needs of young children ages 2 to 6. The benefits of using songs, action poems, and movement activities to teach Bible stories are numerous. The developmental benefits include:

- **Songs**: develop listening, language, vocabulary, rhyming, and memory skills
- **Action Poems:** develop gross and fine motor skills, memory, expression, and listening skills
- **Movement Activities:** develop self-expression, balance, coordination, problem solving, role-playing, gross motor and listening skills
- **Creative Dramatics:** develop language and communication skills, role-playing, listening skills, memory, social skills such as sharing, cooperation, empathy, and identification and expression of emotions

The songs, action poems, and creative movement activities in *Make a Joyful Noise!* are designed to help you teach timeless Bible stories and basic Christian beliefs AND have fun! Be prepared for uncontrolled giggling and falling down laughter! Finger plays and action poems capture children's attention while developing listening and fine motor skills. The catchy lyrics and familiar tunes help children remember the stories. Creative movement activities bring the Bible characters to life and satisfy youngsters' need to move their bodies. By using the activities and suggestions in this book, you will create dynamic Bible lessons that will shape your children's journey of faith. By being active participants, children will remember each Bible story and ultimately understand God's love for them. Your little ones will be moving their bodies and singing the upbeat tunes in no time...they will definitely Make a Joyful Noise!

Suggested uses:

- Sunday schools, Vacation Bible Schools
- Faith-based programs - preschool to grade one
- Parents and family in the home

Tips for Teachers & Parents

Three-year Olds:
- Love to imitate adults. Make sure you demonstrate actions with enthusiasm!
- Are talkative even without an audience. Get their attention with props or puppets before trying to teach a song or poem.
- Can respond to verbal instructions but keep them simple.
- Love to dramatize stories and put words into action. Try an action story to practice listening and gross motor skills.
- Like to use new words.
- Can gallop, jump up and down, and balance on one foot. Try a game that requires galloping around a circle or freezing in place.

Four-year Olds:
- Can be show offs or bossy. Make sure everyone gets a chance to share the spotlight.
- Are big talkers and love to tell tall tales. Let them tell and retell the Bible stories!
- Like group activities, but get impatient in large groups. Teach small groups of 4-5 rather than a large class.
- Like to tease and have a great sense of humor. Have fun with exaggerated body language!
- Enjoy rhyming words. Choose poems with word play or repeating nonsense words.
- Can take turns singing along. Teach a simple song by singing the whole song first, then having children repeat one or two lines at a time.
- Can sing soft or loud, speak in a high or low pitch, and repeat a rhythm. Have children experiment with different voices for different verses of the same song.
- Love to explore musical instruments. Pass them out after you have demonstrated and when you are ready to start the music. Give everyone a chance to play an instrument if they wish.
- Can hop, skip, jump over objects, and stand on one foot. Use action poems and songs!

Five-Year Olds:
- Are sensitive, persistent, and insist on following the rules. They point out, "That's not fair!" Establish boundaries for space and respect for others. Say, "Boys and girls please stay on the carpet and move without bumping into your friends."
- Like adult companionship. Reinforce when they ask for permission or wait. Say, "I will get with you as soon as I finish here. Thank you for waiting."
- Can get silly and wild. Allow for giggles and laughter. Be ready to refocus attention!
- Like to make up their own songs. Encourage them with, "Let's add another verse!"
- Can dress themselves and use tools. Provide appropriate props and costumes so children can create their own skits.
- Can begin to jump rope. Use some poems or songs as jump rope chants.
- Can skip on alternating feet, run on tiptoes, and like to dance. Provide all kinds of music – jazz, folk tunes, rock and roll, classical, and country – and move!

God Made the Earth

Genesis 1

In the beginning when God created the heavens and the earth...

🎵 God Made the Earth

(to the tune of "Here We Go Looby Loo")

God made the earth   *Make a circle with arm.*
God made the sea   *Hands make waves.*
God made the fish   *Make swimming motion with hands together.*

And he made you and me!   *Point to another and to self.*

Chorus:
Here we go looby loo   *All walk around circle in one direction.*
Here we go looby lie   *Reverse direction and skip around circle.*
Here we go looby loo   *Reverse direction and skip around circle.*
And He made heaven up high!   *Stop. Look up and raise hands above head.*

God made the earth   *Make a circle with arm.*
God made the sea   *Hands make waves.*
God made the birds   *Bend arms at elbow. Make flapping motion.*

And he made you and me!   *Point to another and to self.*

Repeat chorus and for each verse choose a different animal and movement.

Seven Days of Creation
(Finger play)

God made you	*Point to child.*
And God made me	*Point to self.*
He made everything you see.	*Point to your eyes.*
On day 1	*Hold up one finger.*
He made day and night.	*Make circular arm motion for sun rising.*
On day 2	*Hold up two fingers.*
He made the blue sky.	*Point to sky.*
On day 3	*Hold up three fingers.*
He made dry land.	*Touch the floor.*
On day 4	*Hold up four fingers.*
He made the sun and moon AND…	*Join arms overhead for sun.*
On day 5	*Hold up five fingers.*
He made birds and fish.	*Put palms together, move like fish swimming.*
On day 6	*Hold up six fingers.*
He made man in His likeness.	*Put hands on head and slide them down to toes.*
On day 7	*Hold up seven fingers.*
He rested, you see.	*Fold hands beside head as though asleep.*
God made you	*Point to child.*
And God made me.	*Point to self.*

Variation: Use the patterns on page 93 to make flannel board pieces to tell the story. As you read the poem, have children place the correct pieces on the board or have them recall the story and place the pieces on the board in sequence.

In the Garden

Genesis 3:1–22

Now the serpent was
craftier than any other animal…

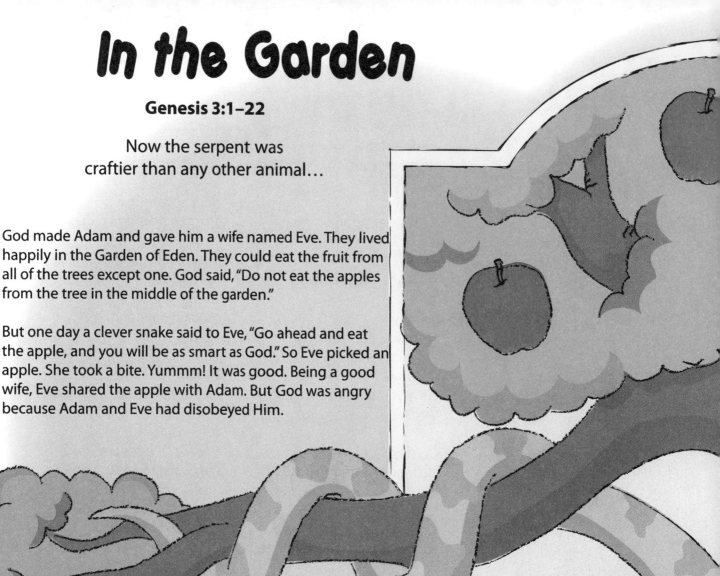

God made Adam and gave him a wife named Eve. They lived happily in the Garden of Eden. They could eat the fruit from all of the trees except one. God said, "Do not eat the apples from the tree in the middle of the garden."

But one day a clever snake said to Eve, "Go ahead and eat the apple, and you will be as smart as God." So Eve picked an apple. She took a bite. Yummm! It was good. Being a good wife, Eve shared the apple with Adam. But God was angry because Adam and Eve had disobeyed Him.

The Apple Tree
(Finger play)

Way up high in the apple tree   *Stretch arms way up high.*
A slithery snake winked at Eve   *Wink.*
Eve shook that tree as hard as she could   *Pretend to be shaking the tree.*
Down came an apple   *Bend to make a downward motion.*
Yummm…it was good!   *Rub tummy and smile.*

Along came Adam, Eve gave him a bite   *Pretend to bite an apple.*
But God was angry at the sight   *Make an angry face.*
Because He had said "Don't eat from the tree   *Cup hands around mouth and yell.*
Adam and Eve,   *Point and shake finger to scold.*
You disobey me!"

So Adam and Eve left the garden together.
And God made the snake
Crawl on his belly forever.

♪ Did You Ever See a Snake?
(to the tune of "Did You Ever See a Lassie?")

Did you ever see a snake, a snake, a snake
Did you ever see a snake
Slither this way and that
Slither this way and that way
And that way and this way
Did you ever see a snake
Slither this way and that?

Did you ever hear a snake, a snake, a snake
Did you ever hear a snake
Hiss this way and that
Hiss this way and that way
And that way and this way
Did you ever hear a snake
Hiss this way and that?

Creative Movement

Preschoolers will have fun pretending to slither on their bellies and move like snakes to music. Or make stick puppets for children to act out the story. Duplicate the snake and apple patterns on page 82 for each child. Have children color and cut out their patterns. Tape the cutouts onto craft sticks to make stick puppets to use with the poem or song.

9

Noah Builds an Ark

Genesis 6:19

And of every living thing, you shall bring two of every kind into the ark…

It was going to rain! God was making a flood to cover the whole earth! But God wanted to save faithful Noah and his family. God told Noah to build an ark – a huge wooden boat – and to gather two of every kind of animal on board. The animals marched onto the ark two by two. Noah and his family got on board last. They closed the door just as the thunder boomed and the lightning flashed. It rained for forty days and forty nights, but everyone in the ark was safe.

 ## All the Rain Is Falling Down
(to the tune of "London Bridge Is Falling Down")

All the rain is falling down, falling down, falling down
All the rain is falling down
And God told Noah…

Wiggle fingers like falling rain.
Shake finger at Noah.

Build an ark with hammers and nails, hammers and nails, hammers and nails
Build an ark with hammers and nails
And build it big and strong.

Pretend to hammer nails.
Throw arms up to show muscles.

March the animals two by two, two by two, two by two
March the animals two by two
And get on board with Noah.

March in place.
Motion with thumb to get on board.

All the rain is falling down, falling down, falling down
All the rain is falling down
But we're safe on the ark!

Wiggle fingers like falling rain.
Wrap arms around body.

Creative Movement

Children benefit from and love using props during songs. Make "All the Rain Is Falling Down" come to life by using the following props. Provide large golf umbrellas for the children to stand under as you make it sprinkle by squirting water from several squirt bottles. As the rain becomes more intense, fully open the nozzle for a downpour of rain. Several children can beat drums and bang cymbals for the thunder and lightning.

10

🎵 The Animals on the Ark
(to the tune of "The Wheels on the Bus")

God said, "Noah, build an ark, build an ark,
   build an ark."
God said, "Noah, build an ark
Before it starts to rain!"

Spoken: And so he did!

All the animals got on board
Two by two, two by two, two by two
All the animals got on board two by two
And it began to rain!

Spoken: For forty days and forty nights!

The pigs on the ark go Oink, oink, oink
Oink, oink, oink, Oink, oink, oink
The pigs on the ark go Oink, oink, oink
Forty days and forty nights!

Additional verses:
The snakes on the ark go Hiss, hiss, hiss...
The cows on the ark go Moo, moo, moo...
The geese on the ark go Honk, honk, honk...
The people on the ark go Up and down...
The babies on the ark go "Waaa, waa, waa…"

Spoken: And then the rain stopped!

God said to Noah, "No more rain.
No more rain, no more rain."
God said to Noah, "No more rain."
And He sent us all a rainbow!

Creative movement stimulates children's imagination and self-esteem. Encourage the children to try the following:
- Move like raindrops falling to the ground.
- Move like a clap of thunder.
- Move like a bolt of lightning.
- Create puddles by having individual raindrops (children) form small groups.

🎵 The Ants Go Marching Two by Two
(to the tune of "When Johnny Comes Marching Home")*

The ants go marching two by two, hurrah, hurrah
The ants go marching two by two, hurrah, hurrah
The ants go marching two by two
The little one stops to tie his shoe

Chorus:
And they all go marching on to the ark
To get out of the rain, BOOM! BOOM! BOOM!

The sheep go marching four by four, hurrah, hurrah
The sheep go marching four by four, hurrah, hurrah
The sheep go marching four by four
The little one stops to shut the door

Chorus

The pigs go marching six by six, hurrah, hurrah
The pigs go marching six by six, hurrah, hurrah
The pigs go marching six by six
The little one stops to pick up sticks

Chorus

The goats go marching eight by eight, hurrah, hurrah
The goats go marching eight by eight, hurrah, hurrah
The goats go marching eight by eight
The little one stops to shut the gate

Chorus

The cows go marching ten by ten, hurrah, hurrah
The cows go marching ten by ten, hurrah, hurrah
The cows go marching ten by ten
The little one stops to say "MOOOOOO"

And they all go marching onto the ark
To get out of the rain, BOOM! BOOM! BOOM!

Creative Movement
March on board the ark to one of these songs and add the sound effects of thunder by banging on pots and pans with wooden spoons. Provide several flashlights to simulate flashes of lightning. The sound of rain can be produced with a rain stick or with plastic bottle shakers filled with rice. Or play recorded rain sounds and have children pretend to use umbrellas to dance in the rain, splash in puddles, and squish in the mud.

12

* Indicates songs and fingerplays featured on the *Make a Joyful Noise!* CD ©2007

🎵 Old Man Noah Had an Ark
(to the tune of "Old McDonald Had a Farm")

Old Man Noah had an ark, E-I-E-I-O
And on his ark he had a cow, E-I-E-I-O
With a "moo-moo" here and a "moo-moo"
  there
Here a "moo," there a "moo"
Everywhere a "moo-moo"
Old Man Noah had an ark, E-I-E-I-O.

Old Man Noah had an ark, E-I-E-I-O
And on his ark he had a pig, E-I-E-I-O
  With a (snort) here and a (snort) there
  Here a (snort), there a (snort)
  Everywhere a (snort)
  With a "moo-moo" here and a "moo-moo" there
Here a "moo," there a "moo"
Everywhere a "moo-moo"
Old Man Noah had an ark, E-I-E-I-O.

Old Man Noah had an ark, E-I-E-I-O
And on his ark he had a horse, E-I-E-I-O
With a "neigh, neigh" here and a "neigh, neigh" there
Here a "neigh," there a "neigh"
Everywhere a "neigh, neigh"
With a (snort) here and a (snort) there
Here a (snort), there a (snort)
Everywhere a (snort)
With a "moo-moo" here and a "moo-moo" there
Here a "moo," there a "moo"
Everywhere a "moo-moo"
Old Man Noah had an ark, E-I-E-I-O.

Snacktime
Provide a snack of animal crackers. To determine each verse of "Old Man Noah," have a child
pull out a cookie from the box!

13

God Makes a Promise

Genesis 9:13

I have set my rainbow in the clouds and it shall be a sign
of the covenant between me and the earth.

♫ God Sent the Sunshine

(to the tune of "You Are My Sunshine")

God sent the sunshine
God sent the sunshine
God sent the sunshine
When skies were gray.

He sent a rainbow
To show He loves you
He'll never take our sunshine away.

Rainbow Streamer Dancing

Children love to move their bodies in creative ways. Try this rainbow dance to get the children moving creatively! Facilitate their creative expression and motor skills by constructing rainbow streamers that they can use as they sing. Tape crepe paper streamers onto a wooden craft stick. Choose colors that are present in the rainbow. Tape one color of the rainbow on each craft stick. Encourage children to work together to move their streamers in the same direction to make a "rainbow" at the end of the forty days and nights of rain.

For even more rainbow fun, tape all colors of the rainbow on a craft stick. Each child will then have his own rainbow. Encourage the children to move their rainbows in creative ways...up high, down low, fast, slow, etc. If you do not have preparation time, delete the craft sticks! Just let the children hold the streamers!

14

Itsy, Bitsy Spider

(Finger play with added verses)

The itsy, bitsy spider
Climbed up the water spout
Down came the rain
And washed the spider out
Out came the sun
And dried up all the rain
And the itsy, bitsy spider
Climbed up the spout again.

Fingers wiggle up.
Fingers wiggle down.
Hands sweep down.
Hands together, then open arms.
Hands sweep upward.
Fingers wiggle up.

The animals on the ark
Sat down for forty days
God sent a rainbow
To make them smile again
Out came the sun
And dried up all the rain
And the animals on the ark
Marched out to play again.

Sit down.
Point to heaven.
Smile and point to smile.
Hands together, then open arms.
Hands sweep upward.
Stand.
March in place.

Creative Movement

How the animals wanted off the ark after forty days of rain and no room to run and play! Try this circle game when your children need to unwind. Gather children in a circle. Have children chant together, "Rain, rain, go away. Little _____ wants to play." Children take turns naming an animal on the ark, then acting like that animal as they run across a finish line. For example: "Rain, rain, go away. Little Piggy wants to play." All the children act like piggies as they run back to the designated "ark."

15

Joseph and His Jealous Brothers

Genesis 37:3-11

Joseph was the youngest of twelve sons. He was his father's favorite. Of course, this made Joseph's brothers very jealous. One day, Joseph's father, Jacob, gave Joseph a special present – a beautiful coat of many colors. This made the other brothers even angrier!

The jealous brothers plotted to get rid of Joseph. They grabbed Joseph and took his beautiful coat. Then they threw Joseph into a deep pit. The brothers decided to sell Joseph as a slave. They took Joseph's coat and covered it with the blood of a goat so that Jacob would think that a wild animal had eaten his favorite son.

Later, Joseph was a slave in Egypt, but Pharaoh made him a governor of the people. Joseph became a rich man. Many years later, Joseph's brothers came to him for help and he forgave them.

🎵 Goodbye, Joseph
(to the tune of "Goodbye, Ladies")

Goodbye, Joseph. Goodbye, Joseph.
Goodbye, Joseph, you're goin' in the well.

Down, down, down, down   *Children all fall down.*

Pray to God, Joseph. Pray to God, Joseph.   *Children get on knees.*
Pray to God, Joseph. Lord, get me outta here!   *Look up, fold hands to pray.*

Up, up, up, up.   *Children stand and march.*

God saved Joseph. God saved Joseph.
God saved Joseph and He'll save you and me!

Creative Dramatics
Young children can act out the story with the following song. Provide the following props: a large shirt, a blanket to throw over Joseph in the well, colored paper in red, orange, blue, purple, yellow, and gold.

 **Joseph Had an Awesome Coat**
(to the tune of "Mary Had a Little Lamb")

Joseph had an awesome coat
Awesome coat, awesome coat
Joseph had an awesome coat
All the colors of the rainbow.

Many colors we can see
We can see, we can see   *Point to eyes.*
Many colors we can see
I see yellow and blue.   *Point to these colors.*

Joseph's brothers took his coat
Took his coat, took his coat   *Pretend to snatch the coat.*
Joseph's brothers took his coat
And threw him in a well.   *Pretend to throw Joseph in
                                                    the well.*

Spoken: And they dipped the coat in the
blood of a goat and took the coat to Jacob.

Many colors we can see
We can see, we can see
Many colors we can see   *Point to eyes.*
I see orange and red.   *Point to colors.*

Spoken: Joseph was sold as a slave.
In Egypt, the king made Joseph a leader.

Joseph prayed to God above
God above, God above   *Look up.*
Joseph prayed to God above   *Fold hands to pray.*
And Pharaoh made him rich.

Many colors we can see
We can see, we can see
Many colors we can see   *Point to eyes.*
I see purple and gold.   *Point to colors.*

17

Baby Moses Is Found in the Nile

Exodus 2:3–10

Long ago, King Pharaoh ordered that all Hebrew baby boys be killed. To save her son, one Hebrew mother put her baby in a waterproof basket and placed the basket in the river. The baby in the basket floated along the river to where the royal princess was playing with her friends. The princess heard a baby crying and spied the basket. When she opened the basket, she spied a little baby. She took him to the palace and gave the baby boy a name. His name was Moses because Moses means drawn from the water.

🎵 Moses in the Water
(to the tune of "Wade in the Water")

Baby Moses in the water
Floating in the water, children
A basket in the water
Carried Moses down the Nile.

Creative Dramatics

Have young children act out the story and pretend to find the Baby Moses in the Nile. Provide a large basket with a baby doll wrapped in a blanket. Provide a crown for the Egyptian princess. (See the crown pattern on page 89.) Have children take off their shoes and pretend they are wading in a river, picking up the baby, and carrying Moses home.

18

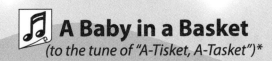

🎵 A Baby in a Basket

(to the tune of "A-Tisket, A-Tasket")*

A-tisket a-tasket
A baby in a basket   *Fold arms to rock baby.*
We found it floating in the Nile
And on the way, we snatched it.   *Bend to grab basket.*

We snatched it, we snatched it   *Make fist. Hold hand over fist.*
Yes, on the way we snatched it
We heard a baby cry, "Waa, waaaa"   *Make fists, rub eyes.*
 And we opened up the basket.   *Make fist. Lay hand over fist. Open.*

A-tisket a-tasket
We opened up the basket   *Make fist. Lay hand over fist. Lift hand.*
And when we looked inside – Oh my   *Peek inside fist.*
We spied a little baby.   *Fold arms to rock baby.*

A baby, a baby   *Fold arms to rock baby.*
We spied a little baby
And Pharaoh's daughter picked him up *Bend to pick up baby.*
And took him to the palace.   *Hold baby and march in place.*

A-tisket a-tasket
A baby in a basket   *Fold arms to rock baby.*
Pharaoh's daughter took him home
And gave the boy a name.

Spoken:
(Was it Abraham?) No, no, no, no   *Shake index finger and head.*
(Was it Isaac?) No, no, no, no   *Repeat.*
(Was it Jacob?) No, no, no, no   *Repeat.*
It was… Moses!   *Cup hands and shout.*

A-tisket a-tasket
Baby Moses in the basket   *Fold arms to rock baby.*

Pharaoh's daughter took him home
And he became a leader.   *Pump arms while marching in place.*
A leader, a leader   *Pump arms while marching in place.*
Moses was our leader
He led us out from Egypt's land   *Look in distance while marching in place.*
And Pharaoh's army chased him.

They chased him, they chased him   *Run in place.*
The chariots, they chased him
Moses held up his right hand   *Stop. Hold up right hand.*
And parted the Red Sea.

The Red Sea, the Red Sea
Crashed down on Pharaoh's army   *All fall down in place.*
Then Moses led the Israelites   *Pause. Get up. March in place.*
Toward the Promised Land!   *All point to door.*

Spoken:
(Was it Abraham?) No, no, no, no   *Shake index finger and head.*
(Was it Isaac?) No, no, no, no   *Repeat.*
(Was it Jacob?) No, no, no, no   *Repeat.*
It was… Moses!   *All cheer and clap.*

* Indicates songs and fingerplays featured on the *Make a Joyful Noise!* CD ©2007

19

God Speaks to Moses

Exodus 3–4

 Moses Saw the Burning Bush
(to the tune of "Here We Go Round the Mulberry Bush")

Moses saw the burning bush The burning bush, the burning bush Moses saw the burning bush	*Hand to forehead looking in the distance.*
While walking in the desert.	*March in place.*
Moses heard the voice of God The voice of God, the voice of God Moses heard the voice of God	*Hand to ear, cock head to side.*
God said, "Take off your shoes!"	*Pretend to bend down and remove shoes.*
Get down on your knees to pray Knees to pray, knees to pray Get down on your knees to pray	*Bend on knee and fold hands to pray.*
For this is holy ground.	*Touch ground.*
Moses thanked the Lord that day Lord that day, Lord that day Moses thanked the Lord that day	*Look up to heaven, hands raised and open.*
For giving him a blessing.	*Put hand on heart.*
This is the way we go to church Go to church, go to church This is the way we go to church	*March in a circle or into the church.*
So early Sunday morning.	

Creative Movement

After sharing the story, have children stand in a circle and listen as you sing the first verse of the song. Have them watch and follow along as you demonstrate the motions. Continue with each verse. Then have children sing the song with you and add the motions. With the last verse, children can march around the room or back inside the church.

Goin' with Moses

(Action chant to "Goin' on a Bear Hunt")

Chorus:	
Goin' with Moses.	*March in place.*
Goin through the desert	
I'm not afraid.	*Point to self. Shake head.*
Look, what's up ahead?	*Hand over eyebrows.*
Verse:	
Hot sand!	
Can't go over it.	*Motion arm as though moving over it.*
Can't go under it.	*Motion arm as though moving under it.*
Can't go around it.	*Motion arm as though going around it.*
Gotta go through it.	*Run in place and say "hot!"*

Repeat chorus after each verse.

Prickly cactus!	
Can't go over it.	*Motion arm as though moving over it.*
Can't go under it.	*Motion arm as though moving under it.*
Can't go around it.	*Motion arm as though going around it.*
Gotta go through it.	*Pretend to climb up and down. Say "Ouch!"*

Chorus

Cave!	
Can't go over it.	*Motion arm as though moving over it.*
Can't go under it.	*Motion arm as though moving under it.*
Can't go around it.	*Motion arm as though going around it.*
Gotta go through it.	*Feel your way in a dark cave.*

Chorus

Feel your way along the wall.	*Move along the wall.*
Oh, oh, What's this?	
Something furry.	
With a long soft thing on its end!	
With sharp things! Big sharp teeth!	
A MOUNTAIN LION!!! Run for your life!	
Run out of the cave!	*Feel your way through the dark cave.*
Whirl through the sand storm!	*Turn around in circles and say "Whoosh!"*
Tiptoe through the snakes!	*Tiptoe carefully and hiss.*
Climb the cactus tree!	*Climb up and down. Say "Ouch!"*
Run through the hot sand!	*Run in place and say "hot!"*
Part the Red Sea!	*Hold hand up in the air.*
We're SAFE!	*Take a deep breath! Say," Whew!"*

21

Let My People Go!

Exodus 7:9–16

Moses said to Pharaoh, "The Lord God of the Hebrews says, 'Let my people go.'"

🎵 Go Down, Moses
(Traditional spiritual)

Group 1:	When Israel was in Egypt's land
Group 2:	Let My people go!
Group 1:	Oppressed so hard they could not stand
Group 2:	Let My people go!
Chorus:	Go down, Moses
	Way down in Egypt's land
	Tell old Pharaoh
	To let My people go!

Creative Movement

Play the following name game to encourage listening skills and practice gross motor skills. Preschoolers will have fun shouting to Old Pharaoh, "Let My people go!" Have one child pretend to be Moses and approach a seated Pharaoh. With the other children seated behind Pharaoh, Moses shouts his request. Pharaoh responds with a name and a motion:

For example, "Mary may go hopping like a kangaroo." Or, "Austin may go swimming like a fish." As more children form behind Moses, they all shout the request until all of the Israelites are free. Allow children to take turns being Pharaoh.

Chased by Chariots

Exodus 14:21–30

When Moses saw Pharaoh's army bearing down on the Hebrews, he did what God told him to do. He lifted up his staff and the waters of the Red Sea parted. What was once the sea became dry land! The Hebrews ran as fast as they could and reached the other side safely. When Moses raised his staff again, the waters crashed down on Pharaoh's army – drowning them all. Moses and the Israelites had escaped. Moses led the people through the desert for forty years in search of the Promised Land.

 ## Wade in the Water
(Traditional)

Chorus:
Wade in the water
Wade in the water, children
Wade in the water
God's gonna trouble the water
God's gonna trouble the water.

Well, who are these children all
   dressed in red?
God's gonna trouble the water
Must be the children that Moses led
God's gonna trouble the water.

Creative Movement
Children remember stories when they have the opportunity to act them out. Because children also benefit from movement, encourage the children to participate in an outdoor game of tag. Half of the group should be "chariots" while those remaining are "Israelites." As the teacher, you will be the "Red Sea." Have everyone stand in a line beside one another. Give the Israelites a head start in running toward you and encourage the chariots to chase them. If they pass you without being tagged they are safe. If they are tagged before reaching you they become a chariot. Repeat this process until all Israelites are chariots.

Creative Dramatics
After singing the song, have children pretend to wade with Moses in the Red Sea. If you can take the children outside on a warm, sunny day, they can have the sensory experience of sand and water play. You'll need a wading pool or a sprinkler and a sandbox.

Tell children that the Israelites followed Moses through the sand in the desert. The Israelites followed Moses through the water of the Red Sea toward the Promised Land. Allow children to take off their shoes and socks and feel the sand between their toes. Ask them to tell you how it feels. Hot? Cold? Smooth? Grainy? Then have children follow the leader to walk through the sand and water and describe what they feel. Allow plenty of time to dry little feet and put on shoes. The sensory experience is one they will remember whenever they sing the song.

The Ten Commandments

Exodus 34:1–24

God told Moses to climb to the top of Mt. Sinai. There, God gave Moses the Ten Commandments. Moses carved the commandments into two stone tablets.

 Ten Little Commandments
(to the tune of "Ten Little Indians")

One little	*Hold up index finger.*
Two little	*Hold up middle finger.*
Three commandments	*Hold up ring finger.*
Four little	*Hold up pinky finger.*
Five little	*Hold up thumb.*
Six commandments	*Hold up index finger on other hand.*
Seven little	*Hold up middle finger on other hand.*
Eight little	*Hold up ring finger on other hand.*
Nine commandments	*Hold up pinky finger on other hand.*
Ten commandments tell us how to live!	*Hold up thumb on other hand.*

Chorus:
Open. Open. Open your Bible.
Read. Read. Read the commandments.
Open. Open. Open your
   Bible.
Read all Ten Commandments.

Repeat chorus.

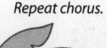

On Top of Mount Sinai
(to the tune of "On Top of Old Smokey")*

On top of Mt. Sinai
Two tablets of clay
God gave Ten Commandments
To Moses one day.

The first commandment
God spoke from above
"Have no gods before me,
Love the Lord as your God."

The second commandment
God's meaning is plain
Speak not in anger
Take His name not in vain.

Keep Sabbath Day holy
Is rule number three
We worship on Sunday
And give praise to thee.

The Ten Commandments
Tell us how to live
We all should follow
These rules God did give.

25

* Indicates songs and fingerplays featured on the *Make a Joyful Noise!* CD ©2007

The Walls Come Tumbling Down

Joshua 6:1–20

Joshua and his army were ready to attack the city of Jericho, but the walls of the city were thick and strong. God told Joshua to march his army around the city wall without a sound for six days. God said, "Do not make a sound except for the sound of the priests' trumpets."

Each day the army paraded around the city in silence. But on the seventh day, the soldiers marched silently, then shouted as loud as they could. The walls tumbled down!

We'll March Around
(Action chant)

We'll march around
We'll march around
We'll march around 'til the trumpets sound!

We'll march around
We'll march around
We'll march around and shout out loud!

We'll march around
We'll march around
We'll march around 'til the
     walls fall down!

We'll march around
We'll march around
We'll march around and
     take the town!

26

Creative Movement
Encourage the children to march around the room or a circle of chairs as they chant the above march.

Joshua Fought the Battle of Jericho
(Traditional tune with added verses)*

Joshua fought the battle of Jericho, Jericho, Jericho
Joshua fought the battle of Jericho
And the walls came tumbling down.

Soldiers marched around quietly, quietly, quietly
Soldiers marched around quietly
And the walls came tumbling down.

Priests blew their shiny horns, shiny horns, shiny horns
Priests blew their shiny horns
And the walls came tumbling down.

Joshua's soldiers shout out loud, shout out loud, shout out loud
Joshua's soldiers shout out loud
And the walls came tumbling down.

Joshua fought the battle of Jericho, Jericho, Jericho
Joshua fought the battle of Jericho
And the walls came tumbling down.

Creative Movement

Young children will enjoy marching and making a loud noise with their trumpets (kazoos) on cue. Designate several children to be the walls of Jericho. Have them stand close, holding their arms way up high in the air to represent the "walls." The rest of the group should march silently around the "walls" six times. After the seventh time around, the children will blow the kazoos, shout out loud, and the "walls" will tumble down to the ground. Repeat this game until everyone has had a turn to be part of the "wall." If you have a small group, designate only one child to be the "wall."

27

* Indicates songs and fingerplays featured on the *Make a Joyful Noise!* CD ©2007

David Stands Up to Goliath

I Samuel 17:19–52

The battle lines were drawn. Goliath dared Saul's army to come get him. Although David was just a young shepherd boy, he decided he could bring down the giant with God's help. After all, God had already saved him from a lion AND a bear. He was not afraid of Goliath because God would help him again. Besides, David knew he was an expert with his slingshot!

Goliath was angry to see that his enemies had sent a boy to fight him. He stomped and fumed and shouted. But David stood his ground. He aimed for Goliath's head and let the stone fly. Zing! Thud! Goliath fell dead. David had slain the giant. There was no battle because the rest of the enemy's troops all ran away.

> **Creative Movement**
> Try this song to develop listening skills and to get the wiggles out!

 Goliath Falls Down
(to the tune of "The Farmer in the Dell" or "The Grand Old Duke of York")

Goliath stood so tall	*Raise hands. Stand on tiptoes.*
He had ten thousand men	*Show ten fingers.*
He marched them up a hill	*March in place.*
And marched them down again.	
And when you're up, you're up	*Reach to the sky.*
And when you're down, you're down	*Touch the ground.*
And when you're in between	*Bend knees.*
You're neither up nor down.	*Stand up. Sit down.*

Then David – he stood up	*Stand up.*
Goliath – he did fall	*Fall down.*
The armies didn't have to fight	*Shake head to say "no."*
'Cause David saved them all!	*Stand and shake hands.*
And when you're up, you're up	*Reach to the sky.*
And when you're down, you're down	*Touch the ground.*
And when you're in between	*Bend knees.*
You're neither up nor down.	*Stand up. Sit down.*

Fe Fi Fo Fum
(Action chant)

Fe Fi Fo Fum Watch out, David Here I come!	*Use a loud deep voice.* *Make large giant steps.*
Fe Fi Fo Fum Look out Giant You better run!	*Use a small high voice.* *Run in place.*
Fe Fi Fo Flee You're much too young To fight with me!	*Use a loud deep voice.* *Hold up fists.*
Fe Fi Fo Foy I'll hurt you with My slingshot toy!	*Use a small high voice.* *Pretend to use slingshot.*
Fe Fi Fo Flared Do you think That I am scared?	*Use a loud deep voice.* *Pretend to bite fingernails as if scared.*
Fe Fi Fo Flone Between your eyes I'll shoot this stone!	*Use a small high voice.* *Point between eyes.*
Fe Fi Fo Flare Go ahead, David If you dare!	*Use a loud deep voice.* *Hands on hips, stand up tall.*
Fe Fi Fo Fling I beat you and Now I am king!	*Use a small high voice.* *Place crown on head.*

Creative Movement: Giant Steps

Try this variation of the traditional game of "Mother, May I?" One child plays "Goliath." The other children line up beside one another about twenty feet away. Goliath selects one of the children and says something like, "Hannah, you may take five giant steps." The child who was addressed then responds with, "Goliath, may I?" Goliath then says, "Yes, you may." Goliath then addresses another child and can change the number of giant steps each time!

The game continues until one of the children reaches Goliath. Whoever makes it to Goliath first becomes Goliath for the next round. Sound simple? It is. In the excitement of the game, however, someone will probably take their giant steps without asking, "Goliath, may I?" When that happens Goliath should remind the player of his or her manners, and the player is sent back to the beginning of the line.

29

Esther Is Brave

Esther 2:1–20, Esther 3–4

A long time ago, the king of Persia was looking for a new queen. All of the most beautiful women in his kingdom were brought to the palace. The king chose a beautiful girl named Esther to be his new queen. No one knew that Queen Esther was Jewish.

At this time in Persia, many people hated the Jews. It was dangerous to be Jewish. In fact, one of the king's men named Haman wanted all Jews killed. Esther had to save her people. She went to the king and told her secret even though she might be killed too. The king had Haman killed instead. Queen Esther is remembered for her bravery.

Creative Movement

Have children dress up like Queen Esther and the king of Persia and have a royal wedding. Provide old sheets, pillowcases, scarves, and ribbons to create royal gowns. Use the pattern on page 89 to make crowns. Children can decorate and wear their own crowns. After the wedding march, children can dance to ballroom music. Play waltzes or lively folk music and have children move slow or fast as the music moves them.

Queen Esther Saves the Jews

There was a brave girl who was beautiful too.
She lived in Persia, but nobody knew…
That Esther was Hebrew and she gave no clue
When the king held a contest for queen number two.

The king of Persia chose Esther as queen.
Then Haman the king's minister came on the scene.
Haman hated the Hebrews and vowed to kill all
Who did not bow down and before the King fall.
Poor Queen Esther! What was she to do?
Would the king spare her life and her people too?

So Esther planned a dinner and asked the king to go.
When Haman said, "Kill them!" Queen Esther said, "No!"
The king had old Haman hanged and then spread the news.
Thus, Queen Esther's remembered for saving the Jews.

Daniel in the Lions' Den

Daniel 5–6

Daniel was taken to Babylon as a slave with many other Hebrew slaves. Although he lived far from Jerusalem for many years, he still prayed to God and he never forgot the Hebrew ways. Daniel was a smart man. He became a very important helper of the king. But when a new king of Babylon ordered everyone to worship him as a god, Daniel refused. As punishment, Daniel was thrown into a pit of lions. Surely, the lions would tear Daniel to pieces! But the next morning Daniel was still alive! God had sent an angel to keep the lions' jaws shut. God saved Daniel and the Babylonians were very impressed.

 ## This Is the Way the Lions Roared
(to the tune of "This Is the Way We Wash Our Clothes")

This is the way the lions roared, lions roared, lions roared
This is the way the lions roared   *Grrrrr!*
When Daniel was in the den.

This is the way the lions moved, lions moved, lions moved
This is the way the lions moved   *Crawl.*
When Daniel was in the den.

This is the way the lions slept, lions slept, lions slept
This is the way the lions slept   *Lie down.*
When Daniel was in the den.

This is the way the lions roared, lions roared, lions roared
This is the way the lions roared   *Grrrrr!*
When Daniel was in the den.

Leo the Lion

(Action poem)

Leo the Lion is the King of the Jungle
And his jaws are big and wide.
When Leo the Lion gives a roar
You better run and hide.

You could hide behind a rock or
You could hide behind a tree
But you had better hide
Where Leo can't see

'Cause Leo the lion is the King of the Jungle
And his jaws are big and wide...
GRRRR!!!!!

Snacktime

Tell children that lions have very powerful jaws. Introduce the word *jaws*. Have children open their jaws wide and roar like a lion. Ask, "What other animals have powerful jaws?" (tigers, sharks, alligators, dinosaurs, etc.) Have children open their jaws and crunch on some animal crackers.

33

Jonah in the Belly of the Whale

Jonah 1:17–31

Jonah was called by God to preach. But Jonah did not listen to God. Instead he ran away. He boarded a ship taking him far away. While Jonah was sleeping, God created a terrible storm at sea. The sailors were so afraid that they woke Jonah up. Jonah knew that God was punishing him. Jonah told the crew to throw him overboard. Then God sent a whale to swallow Jonah up! Jonah lay in the belly of the whale. He asked God to forgive him. Then the whale spit Jonah out and Jonah was washed ashore. He opened his eyes, stood up, and thanked God. Then Jonah went into the town and preached about God.

 ## Five Little Fishies
(to the tune of "Five Little Ducks")

Five little fishies I once knew
Tuna, mackerel, big sharks too
But the one big whale
With the great big hump
He swam by and swallowed Jonah up
Jonah up! Jonah up
He swam by and swallowed Jonah up!

Down in the whale's belly Jonah did go
Gulp! Gulp! Splish! Splash! To and fro
The one big whale
With the great big hump
He swam by and swallowed Jonah up
Jonah up! Jonah up
He swam by and swallowed Jonah up!

Jonah prayed, "God help me please!"
Then that big whale
Gave out a sneeze
Jonah flew out of the whale's blowhole
God had saved Jonah's soul
Jonah's soul, Jonah's soul
God had saved Jonah's soul!

Creative Dramatics
Children can act out the story by banging pots and pans or drums for thunder. Provide fans for the howling wind. The crew rides the waves by bending knees and going up and down as the wind howls and the thunder crashes. Have Jonah pretend to sleep through it all until the crew comes to wake him. When the crew throws Jonah overboard, have him sit down as the children throw a blanket over him to represent being swallowed by the whale. Uncover Jonah. Then have him get up, rub his eyes, and stagger on the beach. Then Jonah kneels down and prays. Everyone says, "Thanks to God!"

34

🎵 Down in the Belly of a Big Ol' Whale
(to the tune of "Three Little Fishies" or "Itty Bitty Pool")*

Down in the belly of a big old whale
Sat Jonah 'cause he wouldn't go and tell
All the people of God's love for them
So, God tipped his boat and made him swim!

Boop boop dit-tem dat-tem what-tem Chu
Boop boop dit-tem dat-tem what-tem Chu
Boop boop dit-tem dat-tem what-tem Chu
Jonah, that whale's gonna swallow you!

When God tipped the boat and made Jonah swim
That whale opened up and swallowed him.
Jonah prayed to God. "Please help me out!"
So the whale gave a sneeze and blew him out!

Boop boop dit-tem dat-tem what-tem Chu
Boop boop dit-tem dat-tem what-tem Chu
Boop boop dit-tem dat-tem what-tem Chu
Jonah flew out with a big Achoo!

Creative Movement
Show photos of fish and whales in the sea. Ask children to name some kinds of fish they know. Ask, "How do fish move?" Have children pretend to be fish – tuna, mackerel, and sharks – and swim to the music. Explain that since whales are not fish, but mammals, they must come up for air. Have each child pretend to be a whale and blow air out of his blowhole.

35

* Indicates songs and fingerplays featured on the *Make a Joyful Noise!* CD ©2007

Mary Rides a Donkey to Bethlehem

Luke 2:1–7

Mary and Joseph had to make the journey to Joseph's hometown of Bethlehem. Although Mary was very pregnant, she made the uncomfortable trip on a donkey. When they got to Bethlehem, there was no place to stay. Mary and Joseph rested that night in a stable with the animals.

 **Mary's Donkey**
(to the tune of "Alice the Camel")*

Mary's donkey has one tail	*Hold up one finger.*
Mary's donkey has one tail	
Mary's donkey has one tail, ride on to Bethlehem.	
Spoken: One more than one is two.	*Hold up two fingers.*
One brown camel has two humps	
One brown camel has two humps	
One brown camel has two humps, ride on to Bethlehem.	
Spoken: One more than two is three.	*Hold up three fingers.*
On the camels are three kings	
On the camels are three kings	
On the camels are three kings, ride on to Bethlehem.	
Spoken: One more than three is four.	*Hold up four fingers.*
Wooly sheep have four legs	
Wooly sheep have four legs	
Wooly sheep have four legs, ride on to Bethlehem.	
Spoken: One more than four is five.	*Hold up five fingers.*
Baby Jesus has five toes	
Baby Jesus has five toes.	
Baby Jesus has five toes, born in Bethlehem!	*Clap hands twice!*

* Indicates songs and fingerplays featured on the *Make a Joyful Noise!* CD ©2007

🎵 Hush, Little Baby
(Traditional, author unknown)

Hush, little baby don't say a word
Papa's gonna buy you a mocking bird
And if that mocking bird don't sing
Papa's gonna buy you a diamond ring
And if that diamond ring gets broke
Papa's gonna buy you a billy goat
And if that billy goat don't pull
Papa's gonna buy you a cart and bull

Hush little baby now, don't you cry
Mama's gonna give you a mountain high
If that mountain top's too cold
Mama's gonna give you the sun to hold
And if at night, sun can't be found
You'll still be the cutest little baby around.

Creative Dramatics

Give each child a baby doll to rock and sing to as you sing. Introduce the word *lullaby*. Preschool children will understand that this song is a lullaby designed to sing a baby to sleep, but they will not know the items mentioned in the song. Create some props to teach the verses by cutting out and mounting on construction paper the pictures of a bird, diamond ring, goat, a wagon or cart, a mountain, and the sun. Allow children to name the pictures. To teach each line, hold up the picture to cue the children. To review, allow children to place the pictures in sequence.

Shepherds Hear the News

Luke 2:8–20

On the night Jesus was born, the shepherds were tending their sheep in the fields around Bethlehem. An angel appeared and told the frightened shepherds the news about the new baby who would be king. The angel said, "You will find the baby wrapped in cloth and lying in a manger." Then the shepherds looked up and saw a host of angels in the sky singing and praising God. Then the angels disappeared, and the shepherds ran to Bethlehem to see the new king.

 Tell the Good News!
(to the tune of "Yankee Doodle")

Mary and Joseph went to town
A-riding on a donkey
Mary had a baby boy
And she named him Jesus!

All the angels sing on high
A king has come to save us
Tell all the world the good news
Our Savior's name is Jesus!

Shepherds watching sheep at night
Looked up in the sky
The angels told the shepherds, "Come
To see the newborn king!"

All the angels sing on high
A king has come to save us
Tell all the world the good news
Our Savior's name is Jesus!

40

sheep

 ## Have You Heard the News?
(to the tune of "Baa Baa Black Sheep")

Baa, baa black sheep	*Do the "sign" for sheep.*
Have you heard the news	*Hold hand up to ear.*
Jesus is born	*Do the "sign" for Jesus.*
King of the Jews!	*Place crown on head.*
Born in a stable	*Pretend to hold and rock a baby.*
Lying in the hay	
Little baby Jesus	
Is born today!	
Baa, baa black sheep	*Do the "sign" for sheep.*
Have you heard the news	*Hold hand up to ear.*
Jesus is born	*Do the "sign" for Jesus.*
King of the Jews!	*Place crown on head.*

Jesus

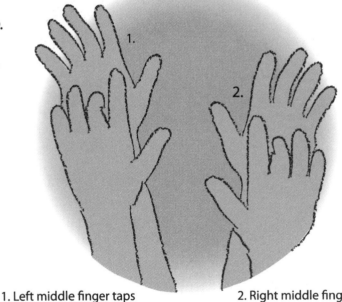

1. Left middle finger taps palm of right hand.

2. Right middle finger taps palm of left hand.

Creative Movement: An Animal Jig

Encourage children to think about what animals may have been present when Jesus was born. What animals have they seen in nativity scenes? Responses may include a donkey, sheep, camel, or goat. Ask questions like, "How do these animals move around? Can you move like a sheep, a camel, a donkey? What would it look like if these animals could dance?" Put on a recording of "Turkey in the Straw" or another lively tune and encourage the group to dance like the animals.

Happy Birthday to Jesus!
(Adapted from a traditional tune by Patty Smith Hill)

Happy Birthday to you
Happy Birthday to you
Happy Birthday, Baby Jesus
Happy Birthday to you!

How we love you
How we love you
How we love you, Jesus
How we love you!

Snacktime
Prepare for a celebration of Jesus' birthday. Bring in or ask volunteers to help supply party hats, plates, napkins, birthday candles, wrapped gifts, and decorations. Ask children, "How old are you?" Ask, "How do you celebrate your birthday? How do you feel on your birthday?" Have children identify each party item. Then ask, "Whose birthday is Christmas Day?" Tell them we want to celebrate another special birthday. Tell children they are going to celebrate Jesus' birthday today. Provide a birthday cake or cupcakes, plastic forks or spoons. Have children count the candles as you light them. Have children sing Happy Birthday to Jesus! Children can help blow the candles out!

 **Go Tell It on the Mountain**
(Spiritual by John W. Work, Jr., c.1907)

Chorus:
Go, tell it on the mountain
Over the hills and everywhere
Go, tell it on the mountain
That Jesus Christ is born.

While shepherds kept their watching
Over silent flocks by night
Behold throughout the heavens
There shone a holy light.

Chorus

The shepherds feared and trembled
When lo! Above the earth
Rang out the angels' chorus
That hailed the Savior's birth.

Chorus

Down in a lowly manger
The humble Christ was born
And God sent us salvation
That Blessed Christmas morn.

Chorus

Creative Movement
Create your own version of the Pony Express to deliver the Good News! Seat children in a large circle outside. Choose two children who are seated side by side. Provide each child with a Christmas card to deliver. Each child must run around the circle in opposite directions and get back to his place and be seated. Play some lively music as children run. Stop the music when one child has arrived back at his destination. Allow time to give all children a chance to be runners or mail carriers if they wish.

Wise Men Come from the East

Matthew 2:1–12

When Jesus was born, three wise men from the East followed a star until they came to Bethlehem. They were looking for the new baby who was to be the king of the Jews. They wanted to bring him gifts of gold, frankincense, and myrrh.

On a Camel We Ride
(Action chant to "Mary Had a Little Lamb")

On a camel, we will ride
We will ride, we will ride
On a camel we will ride
To see the newborn King.

Chorus:
Up and down and to and fro   *Bend knees to go up and down.*
To and fro   *Sway from side to side.*
Up and down and to and fro   *Bend knees to go up and down. Sway.*
It is a bumpy ride!

Spoken: Oops! We fell off!   *All fall down.*
Spoken: Let's get back on our camels now! *Pretend to climb on to repeat the chorus.*

Chorus

Creative Dramatics
Have children act out the three wise men following the star. Provide paper crowns, bathrobes, and wrapped presents. (See the crown pattern on page 89.) Shine a flashlight on a wall to create the star in the East.

♫ Twinkle, Twinkle, Star Above

(to the tune of "Twinkle, Twinkle Little Star")

Twinkle, twinkle little star, how I wonder what you are
Up above the world so high, like a diamond in the sky
Twinkle, twinkle little star, how I wonder what you are.

Twinkle, twinkle little star, wise men follow you afar
From the East they come with gifts, gold and myrrh and frankincense
Twinkle, twinkle let us sing. Kneel before the baby king.

Twinkle, twinkle little king, shepherds come to see this thing
All the way to Bethlehem, in a manger we find him
Twinkle, twinkle little star, Baby Jesus' star you are.

Twinkle, twinkle star above
Jesus is the king of love.

Jesus Is a Lost Child

Luke 2:46–51

Jesus and his parents were in Jerusalem for the Passover feast. But at the end of the celebration, Mary and Joseph discovered that their twelve-year-old son was missing! After three days of searching, they found Jesus in the Temple, talking with the teachers. Mary and Joseph had been so worried, but Jesus was not worried because he was in a safe place.

 **Looking for Lost Jesus**
(to the tune of "Pop Goes the Weasel")

All around Jerusalem
We're looking for lost Jesus
Is he in the temple now?
Yes! Here he is!

All around Jerusalem
We're looking for lost Jesus
Is he in the closet now?
Yes! Here he is!

*For each verse have children guess
a location for the Jesus puppet.*

Creative Movement
Hide a Jesus doll or puppet and have children look for him. Each time Jesus is discovered, choose a new child to hide the puppet.

🎵 Where Is Jesus?

(to the tune of "Oh, Where Has My Little Dog Gone?")

Oh where, oh where has Jesus gone
Oh where, oh where can he be
We're looking for a little lost child
Oh where, oh where can he be?

Oh where, oh where has _____ gone
Oh where, oh where can he/she be
We're looking for a little lost child
Oh where, oh where can he/she be?

Finding Jesus

Children of all ages enjoy playing hide-and-seek. Have the story of Jesus being lost in the temple come to life by trying a variation of this game.

Choose one child to play the role of "Jesus" when he was lost. Choose two children to be "Mary" and "Joseph" looking for Jesus. The remaining children can be "worshipers" in the temple.

Establish boundaries that will serve as "the temple." Mary and Joseph should close their eyes and count out loud to twenty. Jesus and the worshipers should scatter and hide. Mary and Joseph should call "Jesus, where are you?" as they search the temple to find him. They continue searching until they find Jesus. The fun continues until everyone has had a turn to be Jesus, Mary, or Joseph.

47

Jesus Is Baptized

Matthew 3:1–17

One day, Jesus came to his cousin John to be baptized in Jordan River. Many people were standing on the banks of the river. Jesus went under the water. When he came up out of the water, the sky opened and the Holy Spirit came down to Jesus. The people said it looked like a dove above Jesus' head. In a loud voice from heaven, God said, "This is my Son with whom I am very pleased."

Creative Movement
Have children pretend to be baptized by immersion. They can hold their noses and pretend to go under the water as they listen to the following:

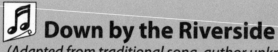 Down by the Riverside
(Adapted from traditional song, author unknown)

I'm gonna lay down my sword and shield	*Lay down pretend sword.*
Down by the riverside, down by the riverside, down by the riverside	
I'm gonna lay down my sword and shield, down by the riverside	
Gonna study war no more.	*Shake finger and head, "No!"*
Gonna put on my long white robe	*Step into robe and pull it up.*
Down by the riverside, down by the riverside, down by the riverside	
Gonna put on my long white robe, down by the riverside	
Gonna study war no more.	*Shake finger and head, "No!"*

Additional verses:

Gonna put on my starry crown	*Put on pretend crown.*
Gonna put on my golden shoes	*Point to shoes.*
Gonna call on my Lord my God	*Pretend to make phone call.*
Gonna shake hands around the world	*Shake hands around the circle.*

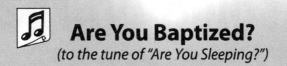

Are You Baptized?
(to the tune of "Are You Sleeping?")

Are you baptized? Are you baptized?
Brother John. Brother John.
Jesus is our Savior. Jesus is our Savior.
Follow him. Follow him.

Repeat, inserting a child's name each time. Older children can sing as a round.

Creative Dramatics

Children may remember seeing an infant baptism in church. Ask them what they remember about the ceremony. Who was baptized? What did the baby wear? Who held the baby? How did the baby become a member of the church family? What sign was made on the child's head with holy water? If possible show photos of a real baptism by immersion. You may wish to take the children to the sanctuary to the baptismal font. Provide a baby doll and have children role-play the baptism ceremony.

Fishing on the Sea of Galilee

Matthew 4:18–20

Jesus' friends Peter and Andrew were fishermen on the Sea of Galilee. One day they came back empty-handed and discouraged. They had fished all day, but they had no fish in their nets. Jesus said, "Go out again and drop your nets." They were not eager to go out again, but they did as Jesus said. What a catch! Their nets were so full of fish that they could hardly pull them in. Jesus said, "From now on I will make you fishers of men." Peter and Andrew left their boat and nets and became Jesus' first disciples.

 ## Fishing for Followers
(to the tune of "My Bonnie Lies Over the Ocean")

Many fishes are deep in the ocean
Many fishes are deep in the sea
Many fishes are deep in the ocean
Oh, bring back some fishes to me.

Bring back, bring back
Oh, bring back some fishes to me (to me)
Bring back, bring back
Oh, bring back some fishes to me.

Jesus is fishing for followers
His follower I want to be
I'm swimmin' to Jesus this morning
'Cause he is so good to me.

50

Creative Movement
Put on some nautical music and have children swim like fish in the sea.

 ## Row Your Boat

Row, row, row your boat
On the Galilee
Bring your poles
Throw your net
Come and fish with me!

Creative Dramatics
Young children can pretend they are fishing from Peter's boat, casting nets and bringing in many fish. This song can be sung in a "round"!

Creative Movement
Make "Row Your Boat" even more fun by providing the children with props to act out the song as they sing. If you wish, provide one or two children with a life jacket to wear as they sit in a blow-up raft together. Model how to row the boat with imaginary oars and begin to sing the song. Use child-sized fishing poles and nets for them to cast as they role-play. A fish pattern is included on page 90 to make "fish" to be caught.

Tip
If you don't have a blow-up raft, create the shape of a rowboat on the floor with masking tape! Or provide several big cardboard boxes. No fishing poles? Just use a yardstick or a dowel rod. No casting net? Use an aquarium net to catch the "fish"!

Snacktime
Provide Goldfish© crackers in small paper cups or tie the crackers up in squares of netting to take home.

Feeding the Crowd

Matthew 14:13–21, Luke 9:10–17

One day five thousand people gathered to hear Jesus preach. After a long day in the sun, the people were tired and hungry. In the crowd, the disciples found five loaves of bread and two fish. Jesus blessed the food and broke it into pieces. He gave it to the disciples and told them to feed the crowd and collect any leftovers! After feeding the five thousand, there were twelve baskets of food left over! Jesus wanted to teach the people to trust God to provide for them.

Creative Movement
Pass the basket for listening and fine motor skills! Bring in twelve different baskets if possible, but one is adequate. Gather children in a circle and play recorded music on a CD or tape player. Stop the music and give one child a basket. Tell children when the music plays, they will pass the basket in one direction. When the music stops, the person holding the basket names a favorite food that they would give to five thousand people. Repeat the routine until all children have had a chance to feed the thousands.

Jesus Fed Five Thousand

(to the tune of "London Bridge Is Falling Down")

With five loaves and two fish, two fish, two fish
With five loaves and two fish
Jesus fed five thousand.

One little child shared his food, shared his food, shared his food
One little child shared his food
And Jesus fed five thousand.

With five loaves and two fish, two fish, two fish
With five loaves and two fish
Jesus fed five thousand.

Jesus prayed and broke the bread, broke the bread, broke the bread
Jesus prayed and broke the bread
Jesus fed five thousand.

Two little fish became a meal, became a meal, became a meal
Two little fish became a meal
For five thousand people.

Gather all the leftovers, leftovers, leftovers
Gather all the leftovers.
And fill up many baskets.

With five loaves and two fish, two fish, two fish
With five loaves and two fish
Jesus fed five thousand.

Snacktime

Provide pita or flat bread in a basket. Allow children to break the bread into pieces to share.
Say a prayer and pass the bread in a basket as they reenact the scene.

How Big Is a Mustard Seed?

Matthew 13:31–32

Mustard seeds are tiny seeds, but they can grow into large, strong trees. Jesus said that the kingdom of God is like the little mustard seed. The seed in each of us can grow into a deep faith.

 How Big Is a Mustard Seed?
(to the tune of "The Muffin Man")

Oh, how big is a mustard seed
A mustard seed, a mustard seed
Oh, how big is a mustard seed
That grows into a tree?

A mustard seed is just like me
Just like me, just like me
A mustard seed is just like me
It grows up big and tall.

My faith is like a mustard seed
A mustard seed, a mustard seed
My faith is like a mustard seed
That's growing every day.

Creative Dramatics
Have children pretend to plant seeds. Provide garden tools and seed packets in the sandbox.

🎵 Little Mustard Seed

(to the tune of "I'm a Little Teapot")

I'm a little bitty mustard seed
I'll grow tall, just wait and see
Plant me in the ground so I can grow
I'll love the Lord and pray just so.

Hold thumb and index together.
Raise hands high overhead.
Bend down to plant the seed.
Fold hands to pray.

My faith is like a mustard seed!

Watch it grow!

Jason
name

Tip

To make "My Faith Is Like a Mustard Seed" nametags or necklaces, duplicate the patterns on page 96 on construction paper. Write each child's name on the nametag with a marker. Cut each nametag out and have the child glue or tape a mustard seed to his or her nametag. If desired, punch a hole and attach yarn to make a necklace to take home.

55

The Good Samaritan

Luke 10:25–37

A man was robbed and beaten and left to die along the roadside. Several people passed by and did not help the injured man. The injured man lay dying when a Samaritan heard his moans. The Samaritan helped the man onto his donkey and took him into town. The Samaritan gave the innkeeper money to care for the injured man until he was strong again. Jesus told this story because he wants us to care for everybody in need, not just friends and family.

Creative Dramatics: To the Rescue Role-Play

Give each child the opportunity to be a Good Samaritan in a disaster simulation. Provide one group of child Samaritans with doctor kits and rolls of adding machine tape to use as pretend bandages. Have another group of children lie on the floor as if they are injured. They can call for help and groan like the injured man. Have the Samaritans go to the aid of their classmates on the floor, bandage their wounds, and help them to their seats.

♫ This Is the Way We Help Our Friends
(to the tune of "This Is the Way We Wash Our Clothes")

This is the way we help our friends
Help our friends, help our friends
This is the way we help our friends
When they wash their clothes.

When they sweep the floor.

When they make the bed.

When they make a cake.

When they wash the car.

When they need a hug.

Pretend to hold and dunk clothes in tub.

Pretend to hold broom and sweep floor.

Pretend to pull the covers up.

Pretend to hold spoon and mix batter.

Palm open. Move hand in circles.

Give a friend a hug.

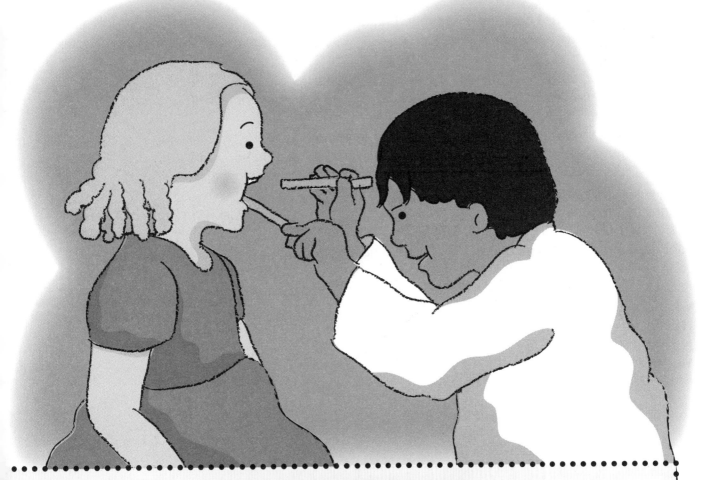

Creative Dramatics: Whose Hat Is It?
In your creative dramatics area, provide hats and costumes for children to pretend to be firefighters, police officers, doctors, nurses, EMT technicians, bus drivers, veterinarians, dentists, teachers, or mail carriers. Have children identify hats or props used by different community helpers.

Build Your House Upon a Rock

Matthew 7:24-29

Jesus said if you have a strong faith, when the rains fall and the floods come, you will be like the man who built his house upon the rock. Your house will not be washed away. Jesus wants us to have a strong foundation of faith so that when trouble comes, we will be strong and trust in God.

🎵 Johnny Works With One Hammer
(Traditional action song)

Johnny hammers with 1 hammer, 1 hammer, 1 hammer
Johnny hammers with 1 hammer all day long.

Hammer with 1 arm.

Johnny hammers with 2 hammers, 2 hammers, 2 hammers
Johnny hammers with 2 hammers all day long.

Hammer with 2 arms.

Johnny hammers with 3 hammers, 3 hammers, 3 hammers
Johnny hammers with 3 hammers all day long.

Hammer with 2 arms and 1 foot.

Johnny hammers with 4 hammers, 4 hammers, 4 hammers
Johnny hammers with 4 hammers all day long.

Hammer with 2 arms and 2 feet.

Johnny hammers with 5 hammers, 5 hammers, 5 homers
Johnny hammers with 5 hammers all day long.

Hammer with 2 arms, 2 feet, head.

What is Johnny building?
He's building his house!
Is it a strong house?
Yes, it's a strong house!

Creative Dramatics
Provide pretend hammers, saws, screwdrivers and power tools in the creative dramatics or block area so children can pretend to build. Add hard hats and create a construction zone with yellow tape to cordon off the area. Children can practice using their "tools" and make the sounds to accompany the song.

🎵 I Will Build My House Upon a Rock

(to the tune of "Polly Wolly Doodle")

I will build my house upon a rock
And pray to God all the day
My house, it is a big, strong house
'Cause I love the Lord all the day.

Make two fists. Pound together.
Fold hands to pray.
Bend arms at elbows. Show muscles.
Hug body.

Fare thee well, Fare thee well
Fare thee well my family
When I go to see my Jesus
Up in heaven he will greet us
And we'll love the Lord all the day.

Wave goodbye.

Look up. Point up with finger.
Shake hands.
Give a hug.

59

Saving the Lost Sheep

Luke 15

Jesus said, "If you had one hundred sheep and lost one, wouldn't you leave the ninety-nine and look for the one who was lost? It will be the same in heaven." Jesus wanted everyone to know that we are like the sheep. God is our shepherd. He wants us all to be saved and go to heaven.

Five Little Sheep
(Finger play)

Five little sheep went out to play   *Hold up five fingers.*
Over the hills, and far away   *Hold hand to eyebrows.*
When the mother sheep went "Baa, Baa, Baa"   *Hands on hips.*
Four lost sheep came running back.   *Move arms like running.*

Continue to count down until there are no lost sheep. Then sing:

No little sheep went out to play
Over the hills and far away   *Hold hand to eyebrows.*
When the mother sheep went "Baa, Baa, Baa"   *Hands on hips.*
Five lost sheep came running back.   *Move arms like running.*

Creative Movement
Young children can count and bring all lost sheep back home. To enhance the children's fine motor skills, give each of them a set of "Five Little Sheep" finger puppets. (See the patterns on page 92.) Tape the sheep to the children's fingers. As you sing the song and the sheep go out to play, cue them to remove one sheep from their fingers. Continue removing sheep throughout the song. Hold up all the sheep when the lost sheep return home.

The Good Shepherd
(to the tune of "The Muffin Man")

Jesus is the Good Shepherd
The Good Shepherd, the Good Shepherd
Jesus is the Good Shepherd
He watches as we play.

Jesus is the Good Shepherd
The Good Shepherd, the Good Shepherd
Jesus is the Good Shepherd
He keeps us safe all day.

Little Bo Peep
(adapted from the Mother Goose Rhyme)

Little Bo Peep
Has lost her sheep
And can't tell where to find them
Leave them alone
And they'll come home
Wagging their tails behind them.

Little Bo Peep
Calls her sheep
She calls their names to find them.
So if you hear
Your name so clear,
Then get in line behind them.

Creative Movement

Play a circle game to gather your sheep and develop their listening skills. Seat the children in a circle and share the story of the shepherd and his lost sheep. Then share the nursery rhyme above. Tell the children that as they all say the rhyme, Little Bo Peep will walk around the outside of their circle looking for her sheep. Choose one child to be Little Bo Peep. At the end of the rhyme, Little Bo Peep calls out the names of a child or two to get in line behind her. The "sheep" follow their leader around the outside of the circle and around the classroom. Continue this listening game until all "sheep" are in line. Have the children follow the leader outside if possible.

Let the Little Children Come to Me

Matthew 19:13–15

Jesus said, "Let the little children come to me, and do not stop them; for it is to such as these that the kingdom of heaven belongs."

Many people came to hear Jesus talk about the kingdom of God. They came to be healed and to tell Jesus their problems. Some people brought their children to be blessed by Jesus. At first, the disciples said, "Go away. Jesus is too busy to be bothered with little children." But, when Jesus heard them, he said, "Don't send the children away. Let them come to me." Jesus hugged the children. He touched their heads and blessed them.

Jesus wants everyone to know that children are important too. Jesus reminds us that the kingdom of God embraces little children, as well as imperfect and even bothersome people. Those who are humble, trusting, and willing to believe as children do will enter God's kingdom.

 **Jesus Loves Me**
(Traditional)

Jesus loves me, this I know
For the Bible tells me so
Little ones to him belong
We are weak but he is strong.

Yes, Jesus loves me
Yes, Jesus loves me
Yes, Jesus loves me
The Bible tells me so.

Creative Movement: Dancing with Jesus
Gather the children on the carpet area or outdoors under a tree. Then ask, "What would you say to Jesus if he were here? What would you want to share with him?" Tell the story and have them act out the scene. Then ask, "Do you think Jesus would like to dance and sing with us?" Put on some upbeat, recorded music and dance with Jesus! Play "If You Love Jesus and You Know It."* Have children clap, stomp, and shake to get the wiggles out!

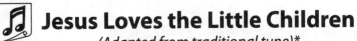

Jesus Loves the Little Children

(Adapted from traditional tune)*

Jesus loves the little children
All the children of the world; Red and yellow, black and white
They are precious in his sight; Jesus loves the little
children of the world.

Jesus wants the little children
To be careful what they do; Honor father, mother dear
Keep their hearts so full of cheer; Then he'll take
them home to glory by and by.

* Indicates songs and fingerplays featured on the *Make a Joyful Noise!* CD ©2007

The Tax Collector Climbs a Tree

Luke 19

When Jesus arrived in the town of Jericho, there were huge crowds of people who wanted to see him. Of course, Zacchaeus, the lying, cheating tax collector, wanted to see Jesus too. But poor Zacchaeus was too short to see because of all of the people lined up along the street. So Zacchaeus thought of a plan. He climbed a sycamore tree and waited for Jesus to pass under the tree. Zacchaeus heard the crowd coming closer and closer and he held on tight.

When Jesus looked up, he saw Zacchaeus in the tree. "Come on down, Zacchaeus," said Jesus. "You can be my friend. Let's have supper at your house tonight." That visit with Jesus turned Zacchaeus' life around. From that day on, Zacchaeus stopped cheating the people. He gave money to the poor. He loved the Lord.

Creative Movement

Little children know what it's like to be too short to see in a crowd! Ask, "Why did Zacchaeus climb the tree? When have you been too short to see or do something? How did that make you feel?" "What could you do to be taller? Could you stand on tiptoes, climb a ladder or a tree, ride on Daddy's shoulders?" Have children tell how they know they are getting taller every year.

Gather children in a circle to teach the song and motions below. Go faster each time as you repeat the chorus.

 ## Head, Shoulders, Knees and Toes
(Traditional action song with additional verses)

Chorus:

Head, shoulders, knees and toes (knees and toes)	*Touch head, shoulders, knees, toes, knees, toes.*
Head, shoulders, knees and toes (knees and toes)	*Touch head, shoulders, knees, toes, knees, toes.*
My eyes, my ears, my mouth, my nose	*Touch eyes, ears, mouth, nose.*
Head, shoulders, knees and toes (knees and toes)	*Touch head, shoulders, knees, toes, knees, toes.*

Zacchaeus climbed a tree (climbed a tree)	*Pretend to climb tree hand over hand.*
Because he was too short to see (short to see)	*Bend down to squat.*
Jesus told him to come down	*Stand. Raise and lower both arms.*
And hand in hand they walked to town.	*Grab a partner and walk around the circle.*

Chorus

I'm growing every day (every day)	*Raise hands overhead.*
I'm growing every day (every day)	*Raise hands overhead.*
Some day I will be big and tall	*Stand on tiptoes. Raise hands.*
And I'll help others who are small.	*Bend down to squat.*

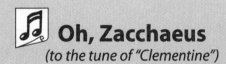 **Oh, Zacchaeus**
(to the tune of "Clementine")

Oh, Zacchaeus, Oh Zacchaeus He was climbing up a tree 'Cause he wanted to see Jesus	*Pretend to climb a tree.*
But he was too short to see.	*Stand on tiptoes, hand to forehead looking for Jesus.*
Oh Zacchaeus, Oh Zacchaeus He climbed a way up high	*Pretend to climb a tree.*
In the sycamore, Zacchaeus waited For the crowd to pass on by.	*March in place.*
Jesus looked up – saw Zacchaeus And he called out to the man	*Look up and point to Zacchaeus.*
"Come down and be my friend forever Come, I'll tell you of my plan."	*Motion with hand to come on down.*
Oh, Zacchaeus, Oh Zacchaeus	
He and Jesus shared some food	*Pretend to eat a meal.*
And Zacchaeus heard the good news	*Cup hand to hear.*
Jesus saves us. God is good.	*Cross hands on chest.*

Creative Dramatics

Have young children line up and pretend to wait for Jesus. Have one child pretend to be Zacchaeus trying to see around the crowd. Have the child pretend to climb the tree, then sit and wait for Jesus. Choose one child to be Jesus and say to Zacchaeus, "Come on down. You can be my friend." Provide play money so Zacchaeus can give it to the poor people in the crowd.

Jesus Enters Jerusalem

Matthew 21:1–11

When the people heard that Jesus was coming into Jerusalem, they lined up along the streets to see him. They put palms and clothing down before him to honor him. They shouted out "Hosanna," or "Welcome!"

Grand Entrance Action Story: Ask children to tell you how they would welcome a friend or visitor to the classroom. Ask, "How would you welcome Jesus to our classroom?" Children may want to shake hands, give hugs, or bow to the guest. Have children listen and make the actions or the sounds on cue as you read the following story, pausing for children to add the sound effects.

Tell children that they are going to add sounds to the story when they hear the characters. Practice making these sounds:

Actions and Sounds
Donkey = "Clip, clop! Clip, clop!"
People = Clap hands.
Disciples = Bow.
Jesus = "Hooray!"
Pontius Pilate = "Boo!"
Roman Soldiers = "Hiss!"

One day Jesus (Hooray!) was on his way to Jerusalem. Jesus (Hooray!) told his disciples (Bow) to find him a young donkey (Clip, clop! Clip, clop!) to ride into the city. The disciples (Bow) found him a donkey (Clip, clop! Clip, clop!) and Jesus (Hooray!) climbed on.

Many people (Clap hands) lined the streets of Jerusalem to see Jesus (Hooray!) pass by. As Jesus (Hooray!) got closer, the people (Clap hands) heard the hooves of the donkey (Clip, clop! Clip, clop!) on the street. The people (Clap hands) laid down palms before Jesus (Hooray!) on the donkey (Clip, clop! Clip, clop!) and shouted "Hosanna," which means "Welcome!" The disciples (Bow) led the way into the city and along the streets.

But not everyone was glad to see Jesus (Hooray!) that day. Pontius Pilate (Boo!) and the Roman soldiers (Hiss!) had been waiting for the king of the Jews. The Roman soldiers (Hiss!) arrested him and took him before Pontius Pilate (Boo!), the governor. The disciples (Bow) ran away. Many people (Clap hands) wanted Jesus (Hooray!) killed. On Easter morning, we remember that Jesus (Hooray!) died for us so we can go to heaven too!

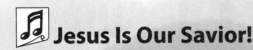

♫ Jesus Is Our Savior!

(to the tune of "She'll Be Comin' Round the Mountain")

He'll be riding on a donkey when he comes
He'll be riding on a donkey when he comes
He'll be riding on a donkey, when he comes into the city
He'll be riding on a donkey when he comes.

We will all go out to meet him when he comes
We will all go out to meet him when he comes
We will all go out to meet him, and we'll lay the palms before him
We will all go out to meet him when he comes.

Shout Hosanna in the Highest when he comes
Shout Hosanna in the Highest when he comes
Shout Hosanna in the Highest! Jesus has come to save us
Shout Hosanna in the Highest when he comes!

Oh, Jesus is our Savior. He's our Lord
Oh, Jesus is our Savior. He's our Lord
Oh, Jesus is our Savior, and we call him the Messiah
Oh, Jesus is our Savior. He's our Lord!

Creative Dramatics

Provide palms on Palm Sunday and have children carry them as they march around singing the song. You can also provide streamers and rhythm instruments to create a parade. Tell children they will pretend to be Jesus riding on a donkey as they enter the classroom (the gates of Jerusalem). When the children enter the classroom, make a grand entrance by having them walk under a canopy of palm leaves held by fellow classmates.

Peter Denies Jesus

Luke 22:31–35

Peter was scared, but he wanted to find out where the soldiers had taken Jesus. As he got closer to hear what they were saying, someone pointed a finger at Peter and said, "You were with Jesus!" But Peter said, "No, you're wrong. I don't know Jesus." Peter lied three times just as Jesus had said he would. Each time a rooster crowed.

🎵 The Rooster Crows Three Times
(to the tune of "Farmer in the Dell")

The rooster crows three times
The rooster crows three times
Cockle doodle doodle doo
The rooster crows three times.

Repeat three times.

Creative Movement

Younger children can pretend to crow like roosters greeting the morning as they strut around the room to music. Facilitate children's love for movement by providing them with props that will transform them into roosters. Give one child a pair of yellow gloves for rooster feet and a red headband for the cock's comb. (See the pattern on page 91 to make headbands and feathers for all children.) Play recorded music and encourage the children to strut as they think roosters do. When the music stops, the roosters freeze!

Creative Movement

All of the children except one sit in a circle facing each other. The remaining child goes around the circle, tapping each child gently on the head and saying, "duck." The tapper continues around the circle until finally tapping a child and saying, "rooster." The child whose head was just touched jumps up and chases the tapper around the circle. The tapper tries to get all the way back to the rooster's spot in the circle without getting tagged by the rooster. If the tapper makes it back to the spot, the rooster becomes the new tapper and the game continues. But if the rooster catches the tapper, the tapper continues his or her walk around the circle. To add a different twist, have the children say "quack" and "cock-a-doodle-doo" instead of "duck" and "rooster."

Jesus Is Risen!

Mary Magdalene and another Mary went to Jesus' tomb. When they arrived, they saw that the guards were gone and the stone had been rolled away from the entrance. They were scared, but got up the courage to go closer. They looked inside the cave only to discover that Jesus' body was gone! Instead of Jesus, the two Marys saw an angel in the tomb. The angel told them, "Jesus is not here. He is risen!" The two Marys ran away to tell the disciples what they had seen.

🎵 Rise and Shine!
(Traditional camp song)

Rise and shine
And give God the glory, glory
Rise and shine
And give God the glory, glory
Rise and shine
And give God the glory, glory
Children of the Lord.

Hot Cross Buns

(Traditional)

Hot cross buns!
Hot cross buns!
One a penny, two a penny
Hot cross buns!

Hot cross buns!
Hot cross buns!
If you have no daughters
Give them to your sons!

Snacktime

Serve traditional hot cross buns, or help children add crosses to sweet rolls. Provide paper plates, paper towels, napkins, one bun per child, and several tubes of prepared frosting. Help preschoolers with their fine motor skills and eye-hand coordination by allowing them to squeeze icing from frosting tubes onto their buns.

🎵 Oh, Happy Day!

(Traditional)

Group 1:	Oh happy day	
Group 2:	(oh happy day)	*Echo in soft voice.*
Group 1:	Oh happy day	
Group 2:	(oh happy day)	*Echo in soft voice.*
Group 1:	When Jesus washed	
Group 2:	(when Jesus washed)	*Echo in soft voice.*
Group 1:	Oh when Jesus washed	
Group 2:	(when Jesus washed)	*Echo in soft voice.*
Group 1:	He washed my sins away.	
Group 1:	He taught me how	
	To watch, fight, and pray	
Group 2:	(fight and pray)	*Echo in soft voice.*
Group 1:	And live rejoicing	
	Rejoicing every day	
Group 2:	(every day)	*Echo in soft voice.*
Group 1:	Oh happy day	
Group 2:	(oh happy day)	*Echo in soft voice.*
Group 1:	Oh happy day	
Group 2:	(oh happy day)	*Echo in soft voice.*
Unison:	Oh happy, happy day!	*Loud.*

72

♫ We'll Make a Joyful Noise!
(to the tune of "Farmer in the Dell")

We'll make a joyful noise
We'll make a joyful noise
We'll blow our horns and beat our drums   *Blow kazoos. Beat drums.*
We'll make a joyful noise!

We'll sing a joyful song
We'll sing a joyful song
We'll sing a song to praise our God
We'll sing a joyful song!

We'll make a joyful noise
We'll make a joyful noise
We'll shake our bells and play our sticks   *Shake bells. Bang sticks together.*
We'll make a joyful noise!

Creative Movement
Provide children with rhythm instruments to make a joyful noise. See the tips on pages 94–95 to make easy instruments.

73

 **Beat Your Drum If You Love Jesus**

(to the tune of "Ten Little Indians")

Beat your drum if you love Jesus
Beat your drum if you love Jesus
Beat your drum if you love Jesus
And shake your tambourine!

Tap your sticks if you love Jesus
Tap your sticks if you love Jesus
Tap your sticks if you love Jesus
And shake your tambourine!

Clap your cymbals if you love Jesus
Clap your cymbals if you love Jesus
Clap your cymbals if you love Jesus
And shake your tambourine!

Shake your bells if you love Jesus
Shake your bells if you love Jesus
Shake your bells if you love Jesus
And shake your tambourine!

74

Creative Movement
See the tips on pages 94–95 to make easy instruments.

 **B-I-B-L-E**
(to the tune of "B-I-N-G-O")

There is a book, a holy book – the Bible is its name-o
B-I-B-L-E
B-I-B-L-E
B-I-B-L-E
The Bible is its name-o.

In Genesis, God sent a flood and Noah built an ark-o
(Clap)-I-B-L-E
(Clap)-I-B-L-E
(Clap)- I-B-L-E
The Bible is its name-o.

In Exodus, from Egypt land, ol' Moses led the people
(Clap)-(Clap)-B-L-E
(Clap)-(Clap)-B-L-E
(Clap)-(Clap)-B-L-E
The Bible is its name-o.

Matthew, Mark, and Luke and John are chapters in the Bible
(Clap)-(Clap)-(Clap)-L-E
(Clap)-(Clap)-(Clap)-L-E
(Clap)-(Clap)-(Clap)-L-E
The Bible is its name-o.

The Bible tells of Jesus' love and how he came to save us
(Clap)-(Clap)-(Clap)-(Clap)-E
(Clap)-(Clap)-(Clap)-(Clap)-E
(Clap)-(Clap)-(Clap)-(Clap)-E
The Bible is its name-o.

Spoken: Come to think of it, the Bible is the Good News!

The Bible is the holy book that tells us the Good News-o
(Clap)-(Clap)-(Clap)-(Clap)-(Clap)
(Clap)-(Clap)-(Clap)-(Clap)-(Clap)
(Clap)-(Clap)-(Clap)-(Clap)-(Clap)
The Bible is Good News!

♫ If You Love Jesus and You Know It

*(Traditional action song)**

If you love Jesus and you know it, clap your hands.
(Clap, clap)
If you love Jesus and you know it, clap your hands.
(Clap, clap)
If you love Jesus and you know it, then your face will surely show it.
If you love Jesus and you know it, clap your hands.
(Clap, clap)

If you love Jesus and you know it, stomp your feet.
(Stomp, stomp)…

If you love Jesus and you know it, shout "Amen!"
(Amen!)…

If you love Jesus and you know it do all three.
(Clap, clap, stomp, stomp, Amen!)…

76

When the Saints Go Marching In

(Traditional, author unknown)

Oh, when the saints go marching in
Oh, when the saints go marching in
Lord, how I want to be in that number
When the saints go marching in.

And when the sun begins to shine
And when the sun begins to shine
Lord, how I want to be in that number
When the sun begins to shine

Oh, when the saints go marching in
Oh, when the saints go marching in
Lord, how I want to be in that number
When the saints go marching in.

Oh, when the trumpet sounds its call
Oh, when the trumpet sounds its call
Lord, how I want to be in that number
When the trumpet sounds its call!

 **Father Abraham**

(Traditional action song)

Father Abraham had many sons
Many sons had Father Abraham
I am one of them and so are you
So let's all praise the Lord
Right arm!   *Clench fist, bend and extend arm.*

Father Abraham had many sons
Many sons had Father Abraham
I am one of them and so are you
So let's all praise the Lord
Right arm, left arm!   *Add left arm in same motion as right.*

Father Abraham had many sons
Many sons had Father Abraham
I am one of them and so are you   *So let's all praise the Lord.*
Right arm, left arm, right foot!   *Add right foot stepping up and down.*

Father Abraham had many sons
Many sons had Father Abraham
I am one of them and so are you
So let's all praise the Lord
Right arm, left arm, right foot, left foot!   *Add left foot stepping up and down.*

Father Abraham had many sons
Many sons had Father Abraham
I am one of them and so are you
So let's all praise the Lord
Right arm, left arm, right foot, left foot
Chin up!   *Add head nodding up and down.*

Father Abraham had many sons
Many sons had Father Abraham
I am one of them and so are you
So let's all praise the Lord
Right arm, left arm, right foot, left foot
Chin up, turn around!   *Add turning in place continuing other motions.*

Father Abraham had many sons
Many sons had Father Abraham
I am one of them and so are you
So let's all praise the Lord
Right arm, left arm, right foot, left foot
Chin up, turn around, sit down!   *Sit down.*

Ain't It Great to Know Jesus?

*(to the tune of "Boom! Boom! Ain't It Great to Be Crazy?")**

Boom! Boom!
Ain't it great to know Jesus?
Boom! Boom!
Ain't it great to know Him?
He died for our sins to be washed away!
Boom! Boom!
Ain't it great to know Jesus?

Boom! Boom!
Ain't it great to be saved?
Boom! Boom!
Ain't it great to be saved?
We will go to heaven one day!
Boom! Boom!
Ain't it great to be saved?

Boom! Boom!
Ain't it great to know Jesus?
Boom! Boom!
Ain't it great to know Jesus?
He died for our sins to be washed away!
Boom! Boom!
Ain't it great to know Jesus?

79

He's Got the Whole World in His Hands

*(Traditional action song)**

Chorus:

He's got the whole world in His hands
Hands together overhead.

He's got the whole world in His hands
Open hands, palms up.

He's got the whole world in His hands
Hands together overhead.

He's got the whole world in His hands!
Open hands, palms up.

He's got the itty, bitty baby in His hands
Fold arms to rock the baby.

He's got the itty, bitty baby in His hands
Fold arms to rock the baby.

He's got the itty, bitty baby in His hands
Fold arms to rock the baby.

He's got the whole world in His hands!
Hands together overhead. Open palms.

Repeat chorus after each verse.

Additional verses:

He's got the mommies and daddies in His hands…
Hands on hips, twist at waist for mommies.
Show muscles for daddies.

He's got you and me, Brother, in His hands…
Point to you and me.

He's got you and me, Sister, in His hands…
Point to you and me.

80

🎵 This Little Light of Mine
*(Traditional)**

This little light of mine, I'm gonna let it shine
This little light of mine, I'm gonna let it shine
This little light of mine, I'm gonna let it shine
Let it shine, let it shine, let it shine!

Additional verses:
Hide it under a bushel, NO! I'm gonna let it shine…

All around the neighborhood, I'm gonna let it shine…

Don't let Satan pfft- it out! I'm gonna let it shine…

Let it shine 'til Jesus comes. I'm gonna let it shine…

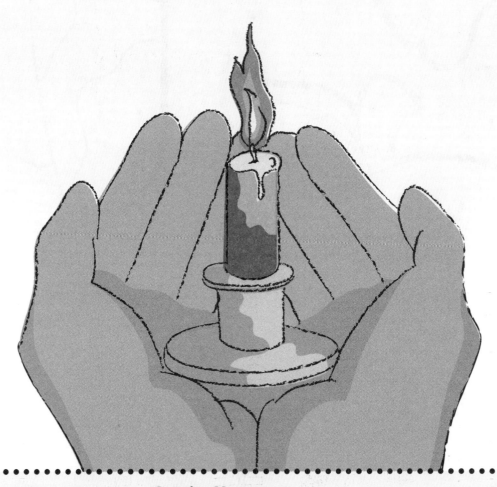

Creative Movement

Have children sit in a circle and play Pass the Light. Play a recorded version of the song and have children pass a flashlight. When the music stops, the child holding the light can shine the flashlight on another child and name the friend. This friend holds the flashlight and begins to pass it around when the music resumes.

81

* Indicates songs and fingerplays featured on the *Make a Joyful Noise!* CD ©2007

Apple and Snake Patterns

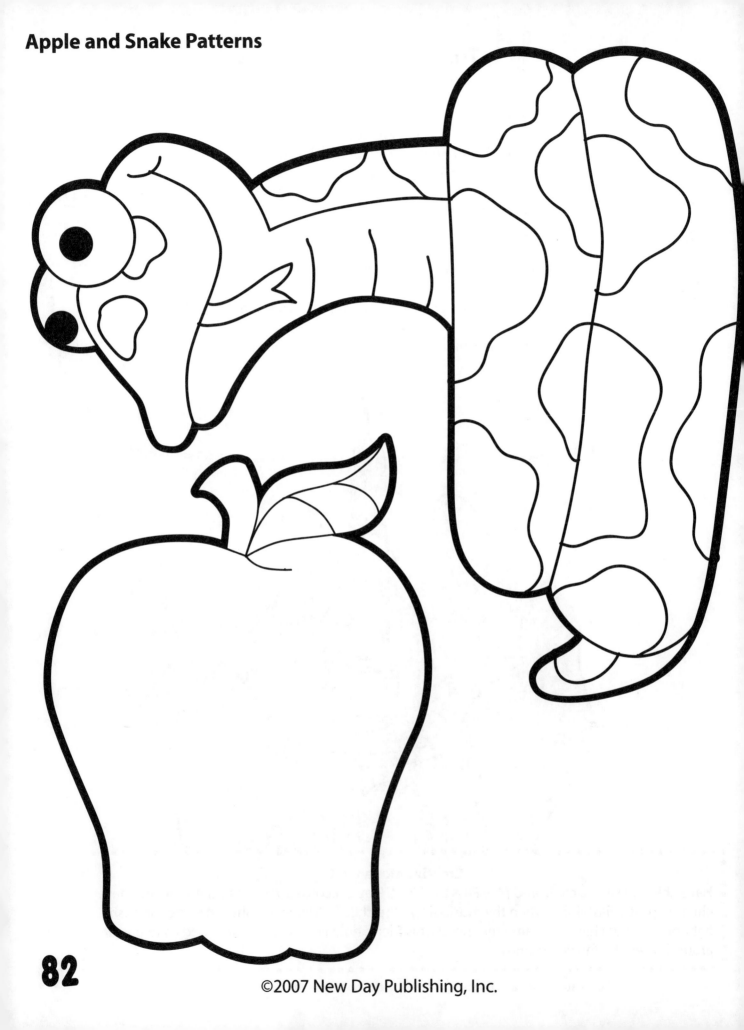

82

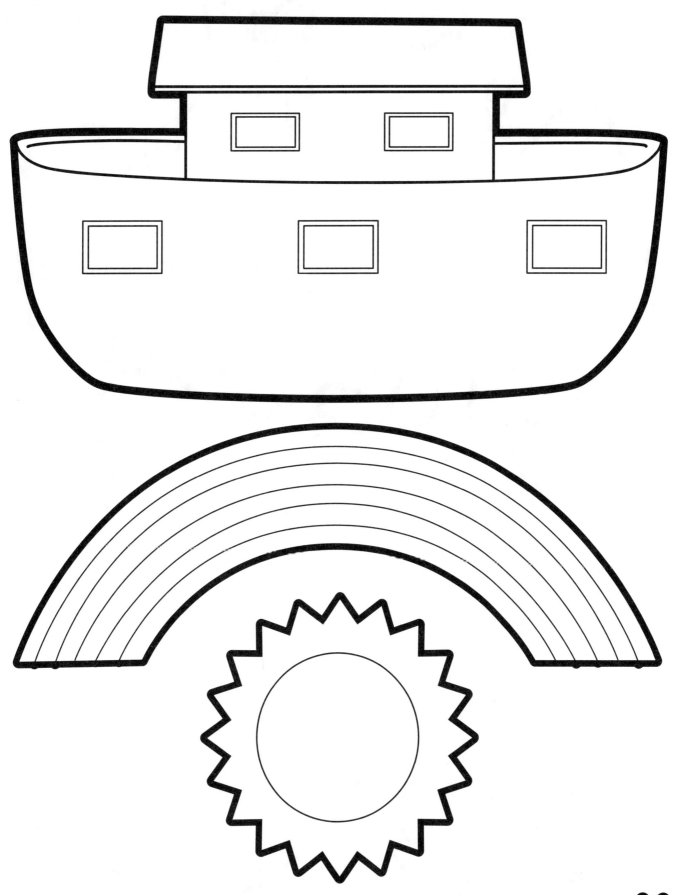

83

Animal Patterns

85

Whale Pattern

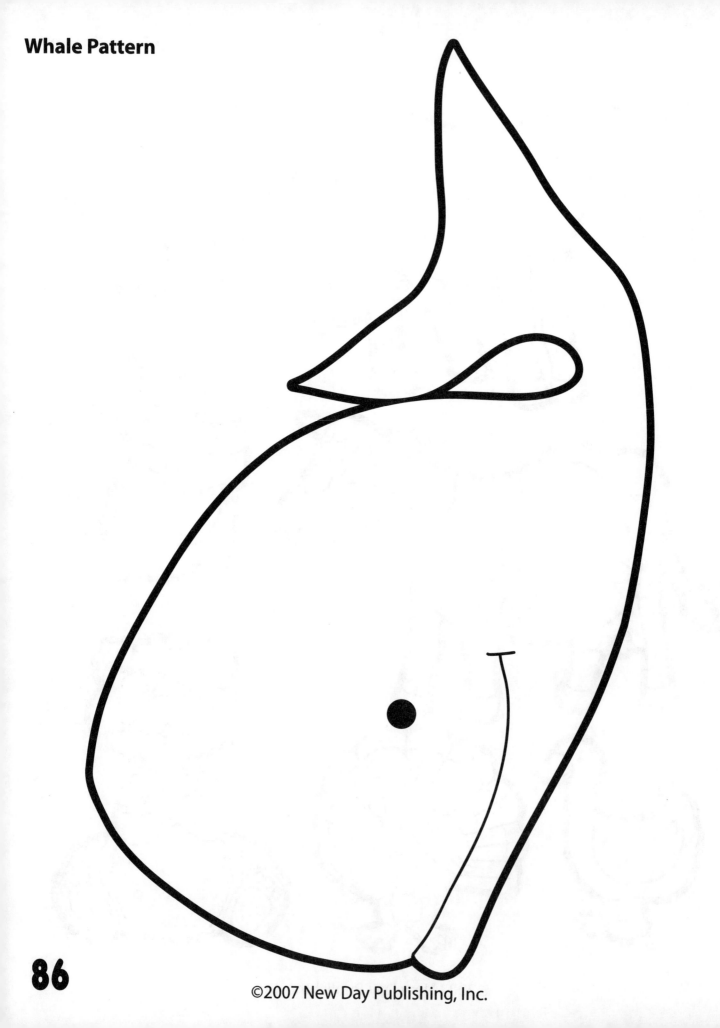

86

Donkey Pattern

87

Camel Pattern

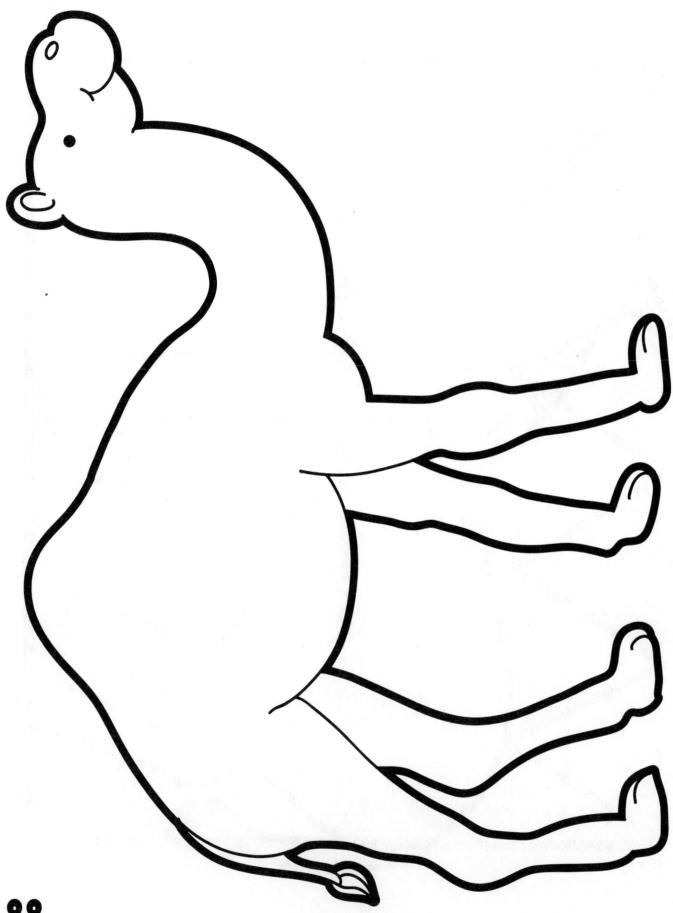

Star and Fish Patterns

90

93

Instruments Made Easy!

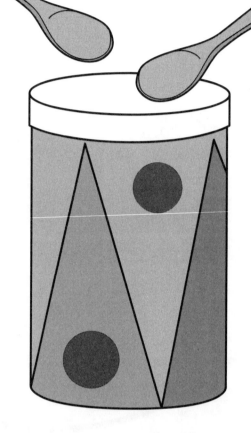

Drums

An empty oatmeal container can be transformed into a drum easily. Cover the outside of the container with colorful contact paper or felt. You can use a wooden spoon for the drumstick. If the spoon is small enough it can be stored in the container.

Shakers

Collect various sizes of clean, plastic soft drink or water bottles to serve as your shakers. Remove the wrappers from the bottles. For variation in tone and pitch, fill each one with a handful of something different like dried beans, rice, rocks, plastic confetti, paper clips, etc. Glue the tops on and secure with tape.

Tambourine

Use two aluminum pie tins for an easy-to-make tambourine. Punch holes in the edges of each so they line up with one another. Attach jingle bells to pipe cleaners and lace the pipe cleaners through the punched holes, joining the pie tins together. Easy!

Sand Blocks

Cover one side of two wooden blocks with sandpaper using glue. Screw a drawer handle to the other side of the block. Children rub blocks together to make a "cha-cha" noise.

Sticks

Cut a dowel rod into equal parts. Paint the rods and use as percussion sticks. Children bang sticks together to the rhythm.

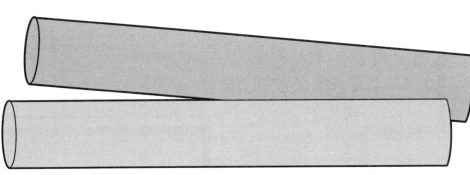

95

Mustard Seed Nametags

My faith is like a
mustard seed!

Watch it grow!

Tape
seed here.

name

My faith is like a
mustard seed!

Watch it grow!

Tape
seed here.

name

My faith is like a
mustard seed!

Watch it grow!

Tape
seed here.

name